MEMORY LANE

COUNTRY ROADS #1

BROOKLYN BAILEY

This is a work of fiction. Names, characters, businesses, places, events, and incidents are either the products of the author's imagination or used in a fictitious manner. Any resemblance to actual persons, living or dead, or actual events is purely coincidental.

Any trademarks, service marks, product names, or named features are assumed to be the property of their respective owners and are used only for reference. There is no implied endorsement.

Memory Lane, Country Roads #1
Copyright © 2022 Brooklyn Bailey
All rights reserved.

Cover Design by Germancreative on Fiverr

Paperback ISBN-13: 979-8-9864529-4-4

 Created with Vellum

ENHANCE YOUR READING

To Enhance Your Reading of Memory Lane read the Trivia Page near the end of the book prior to opening chapter #1.

No Spoilers—I promise.

Check out my Pinterest Boards for The Country Roads Series & its characters.

DEDICATION

To all my high school classmates that remain in our hometown. Years and parenthood led me to see what you always knew.

Special thanks to my family for letting me live my dream even if it means I am writing all night.
If you were a book, you'd be a BEST SELLER.

ONE

Athens has only two stoplights, one of the 4,724 reasons I want to leave this town.

I GLANCE at the dashboard clock. I'm twenty minutes earlier than usual. Although I'm sitting at a red light now, I know stoplights won't help me pass the time.

Athens is a quintessential small, rural town. My mother was born and raised here. My father was born and raised here. As were their parents and most of the town's population. 'The Locals', as I like to refer to them, love everything about Athens. They plan to always stay in Athens—this is not my goal.

When the light turns green, I decide to treat myself to breakfast as I don't have anything else to do. I pull into the busy parking lot of our one and only grocery store. I prefer the store's bakery department donuts over gas station pastries. My stomach growls as I exit the car. Maybe I will allow myself two donuts this morning.

Breakfast is not a meal I usually consume. I enjoy my lunch, dinner, and snacks in between. I'm not a morning person, and usually don't allow myself time for breakfast. I pay for my donuts and milk to wash them down, then I return to my car. I enjoy one sweet pastry ring before exiting the grocery parking lot.

TWO

The grocery selection is limited to the tiny grocery store and two gas station/convenience stores. This is one of the 4,724 reasons I want to escape this town.

I PARK beside Adrian in the high school parking lot.

"Madison, you're early," Adrian greets. When she lowers her squeaking tailgate, we hop up to await the arrival of the rest of our group of friends. The metal is cool against my thighs at the hem of my shorts. I'm glad I didn't wear the sundress I had laid out for today. Kicking my legs forward and back, I glance at Adrian's cell phone as she sets a reminder for after school. Her calendar for the day is cluttered from 3:30 on. I smile, loving that her dream of owning her own business is coming to fruition.

"I had a craving for donuts." I explain my early arrival.

She's no fool. She knows about my mom and home life. She knows I needed to escape. I attempt to put the focus back on her. "Why are you so early?"

"I'm having trouble sleeping. All I can think about is opening my shop." She can't subdue her wide smile. "I'm constantly making notes and jotting down ideas. Would you like to go with me to garage sales in the morning before school? I need to start gathering inventory."

For three months she's focused on paperwork, city and state forms for licenses, opening bank accounts, and securing a storefront for her resale shop. She recently set her tentative opening date, and now she's afraid she won't have the inventory she needs to open.

"Before school?"

"I've mapped out a few garage sales that open tonight at 5:00. Troy and Bethany plan to go to them with me. I've found four that open between 6 and 7:30 in the morning." My interest grows as she explains. "We'll just look for anything I can turn a profit on and leave my name and number for anything they have left over when they close their sale."

"If you provide the donuts and caffeine, I'll join you."

Adrian wraps me in an embrace while thanking me. I've already helped quite a bit in the planning stages, and I will continue to assist as she opens. Adrian opens her Notes App, then lists her upcoming tasks with me. All eight of us assist her as best as we can. Winston, and I are the most involved. Winston through his involvement in his family's theater, knows more about the business side of things. I'm a planner and creative helper. Adrian chose one of my ideas to name her shop.

"Next Thursday and Friday are free trash pick-up days in Athens," I mention. "We should pair up in teams of two with the trucks, divide the town, and pillage each morning and afternoon. I've seen everything from furniture to clothes sitting on the curb in years past."

"That's a fabulous idea."

I offer to plan our attack and direct the group for Adrian. A knowing smirk graces her face. She's very aware I will plan the outing as if I'm preparing an army at war.

"So, how was the rest of your night with Canton? I can't believe the two of you ducked out of the movie before the halfway point." I elbow her.

Adrian sighs deep before reliving an encounter she seems to have forgotten in less than twelve hours. "He may be eye-candy, but Canton is lacking, if you know what I mean."

"Seriously Adrian, you are so hard on guys. Nobody is perfect, even you."

"Please." She begins to explain her rating system. "When he kisses, his lips and mouth are too soft. They are like wet spaghetti noodles. He likes to lick and not in a hot, turn-me-on way. He's like a cow at the salt block. He's a wham-bam man." A shiver of revulsion quakes through her. It was all I could do to pretend it was fun when we parted ways."

I shake my head at her. "You probably scared the poor guy. You know not all men want a dominant woman."

"I wish I would have stayed for the whole movie and parted ways alone when you did."

We joke about the night a bit more. Adrian notices my eyes focus on the far corner of the lot. She turns her head to find Hamilton and Troy approaching in their trucks. Within minutes, all nine of us will be here, visiting, joking, and dreaming of our graduation only a week away.

Adrian asks, "Mind if I share a few things with you to see what you think?" When I nod, she begins. She scrolls through her cell phone for her Notes app to share with me. "I thought I would open the store 11 to 6 on Wednesday through Saturday. I'd be available 4 to 6pm on Saturday, Monday, and Tuesday for the community to drop off items they no longer want. Then, I could use Mondays and Tuesdays to prep the items, display them in the store, or work on updates to social media and advertising." Adrian anxiously looks to me for input.

"I like it. I'm glad you planned times the store is closed for you to get stuff ready. I worried you might try to help customers while you worked on new items, stretching yourself too thin." I nod decisively. "I think this schedule will work."

I hope my words are exactly what she needs to keep her motivated. Adrian squeezes my hand in thanks. My friend is a strong, competent woman. I know she will rock at running her own business. She knows she can do it. With opening day drawing near, she's faltering a bit in her confidence of her abilities. I attempt to provide her with affirmation that she can do this.

THREE

There are only three chain restaurants in town: Pizza Hut, McDonald's, and Hardee's. Yet another of the 4,724 reasons I want to escape Athens.

AS TROY and Bethany pull next to Adrian in the small parking lot behind her future resale shop, I wave. She's surprised to see me in the cab of the truck with them. I said nothing about helping her tonight. She thought we only had plans for the morning.

"Surprise!" I shout as I exit from the cab.

"Madison, what are you doing here?" she asks, thrilled I tagged along. "Are you really so bored that you want to visit garage sales on a Thursday evening?"

"Not bored. I come bearing gifts." I extend my hand, which contains a little, rectangular box, towards Adrian.

Her fingers fumble a bit trying to open the packing tape, causing Troy to offer his pocket knife. When she lifts the lid, she finds business cards. A gasp of excitement escapes her lips as she pulls out the first card. A large, bold font greets her near the top. "Gingham Frog Repurposed Treasures." Her business is typed in black to share with everyone. Her shop's address, her cell phone number, and a website domain are present.

"I don't have a website." Adrian's brow furrows, and she chews on her lower lip. She feels bad for pointing out the error.

"I'm currently creating it for you. Winston and I have been working on it for a few weeks already. Turn it over."

She flips the business card over in her hand. On the back it reads, "Please feel free to drop off or call for a pickup of any items that remain at the end of your sale."

I explain, "Tonight, and in the morning, you can leave these at each garage sale. I thought maybe you'd get inventory this way."

I planned ahead and secured business cards; I'm sure Adrian is mentally kicking herself for not thinking of it.

"Okay," Troy interrupts. "Let's get going. Inventory won't magically appear on your shelves." We pile into the crew cab of Troy's old Ford truck, and Adrian directs him towards the first garage sale address.

FOUR

No need to call for references when an applicant applies for a job; everyone knows everyone. This is one of the 4,724 reasons I want to escape this town.

IN MY HAND, I clutch the letter I've been anxiously awaiting since mid-April. It seems so long ago that Hamilton drove with me to Columbia, Missouri. visiting with the baseball coach and team while I sat through a few exams. I'm nervous now as the contents of this envelope might speed up my studies at college.

I choose to open the letter in my favorite place. I tuck it into my short's pocket, then grab a bottle of water for my walk. From the front yard, I cross the gravel road, and walk through the cow pasture on the gentle path among the green ground cover. I'm the only one to venture this way; my many trips have created this narrow path.

It only takes ten minutes to find my secluded spot. Large trees surround the fenced area. I easily climb over the chain-link fence that protects the forty-two weathered headstones. I find this old, forgotten cemetery peaceful. Those that lie here intrigue me. I've often imagined the lives they've led and families they left behind.

In summers past, I took photos of each headstone then used the internet to see if I could uncover any information on them. In my research, I found some relatives on ancestry sites. They were grateful for the photos I shared and the address of the final resting place of those they desperately searched to connect with.

I choose to sit near my favorite headstone belonging to W. Taul with dates of 1840-1899. Slowly, I slide my finger under the edge and tear the envelope open. I pull the letter out. As I unfold it, I browse the information one time then read it more thoroughly the second. The scores are high enough to test out of 12 college hours. I tip my head to the sky and whisper a prayer of thanks to Heaven.

My excitement is not that my tuition will be greatly lowered but that my time spent obtaining my diploma shrinks. With the 48 hours I completed while in high school and during summer classes, these 12 CLEP hours allow me to start as a junior this fall. I will only need two years to become a teacher. It's not that I plan to hurry back to Athens. I am not sure where I will decide to teach—I am anxious to start earning money that will allow me to start my new life away from this small town.

FIVE

You can't try to sneak into a bar or buy alcohol while underage—they know your age, they know your parents, or they know your family. This is one of the 4,724 reasons I want to leave Athens.

FRIDAY MORNING, after visiting three garage sales, Adrian drives me back to the high school lot. I smile noting we are the last to arrive. Hamilton and Latham have lowered their tailgates, Salem, Savannah, Winston, Troy, and Bethany sit beside them or stand nearby. I'm barely out of the truck when Bethany calls for us to hurry.

"We found a house to rent," Troy's masculine voice greets as he squeezes Bethany, who is tucked at his side. Perpetually touching, she has her right hand tucked in his back pocket and her left on his chest.

I'm not shocked. They've been planning on finding a place to live together since junior year. Their parents support it, and they already act like a married couple. In our group of nine, they are the only two that dated each other through high school. I love my group of eight friends standing here with me and can't wait to see what the years following graduation hold for us.

Recently, Senior Prom added a second couple to our group as Latham asked to escort Salem as friends. That night and the days that followed surprised them as much as the rest of us. They claim sparks flew, and they tried to deny them while holding each other. Considering they were kissing on the dance floor by the last song of the evening, they didn't struggle long against the pull they claim to have suddenly felt. I assume they had feelings for each other prior to the dance, but they emphatically deny it. I just find it hard to accept they'd been around each other for the past four years in our group then suddenly one night while dressed to the nines, surrounded by balloons and streamers, in the dim lighting of the high school gym, with music playing that BAM something ignited between them. I don't buy it.

I'm reminded of a recent conversation with Adrian. She stated our little clan seems to be infatuated with pairing up. When she claimed Salem and Latham were twitterpated with one another while batting her eyelashes, I claimed it's the circle of life in this small town; residents are born, grow up, graduate, marry, work, start a family, and die here. It's just another of the reasons I need to leave Athens, and the sooner the better. I smile know as I realize we quoted from *Bambi* and *The Lion King*.

My thoughts return to the present. Bethany's sweet smile conveys her love and utter happiness to begin life after graduation with the man of her dreams. "The living room is big enough to have you all over. You're welcome anytime to drop by and hang out."

"Well..." Troy draws out the word before whispering in Bethany's ear. She giggles and swats at his chest while a blush creeps upon her face.

"We all promise to text or call prior to showing up," I promise, hoping to avoid Troy announcing what they might be doing sometimes if we just drop in. Everyone nods in agreement.

"We'll throw a big housewarming bash when we get moved in the Monday after graduation," Troy announces. "And our house will be party central. No need to worry about getting caught in public with alcohol." He beams proudly.

SIX

Everyone drives pick-up trucks in Athens, another of the 4,724 reasons I want to escape this town.

TODAY IS THE DAY. Adrian gets to meet the realtor at 11:00 a.m. She gets the keys and will officially be leasing her store space. Weeks of paperwork and filing forms with the city and state led to this. I guess she's already a business owner on paper, but with keys in hand she can begin working on the physical space.

"Good morning," she greets me immediately, cheer clear in her voice. "Today's the big day."

"How are you feeling?" I ask, knowing her excitement must be at an all-time high.

"Eleven o'clock can't get here fast enough. I'm running out of things to keep me busy. I've cleaned my room, folded a load of laundry, eaten breakfast, walked our dog, showered, dried and styled my hair, but it's only 9:15."

"I'm on my way to town," I state. "Want to meet somewhere? I could distract you for a bit."

"Okay. Where?"

"The Blue Jays are practicing. We could sit and watch."

We agree to meet at the park; I need to be with her. I want to share in her excitement.

Adrian backs into a shaded spot beside my car. We meet at the rear and simultaneously hop to sit on her tailgate.

"I always feel like a stalker, a wanna-be girlfriend, and a pervert sitting in my car watching them practice." I smile at Adrian before scanning the action on the baseball field.

"After four years, I'm sure everyone in town knows what a devoted fan you are of the Blue Jays." She squeezes my forearm. "I'm sure the newbies see the older players wave and call to you. They'll figure it out soon enough."

"I won't be able to get away with this at college this fall." I don't pull my eyes from the field and players. "I'll have class, and they have closed practices. I'm gonna have withdrawals." I wave at Hamilton as he runs a lap around the outside of the field. He's not surprised we are here. In fact, I'm sure the team would worry if I didn't pop in on practices. They'd probably text or call to check on me.

I hop off the tailgate, retrieve bottles of water from my backseat. Adrian holds my water bottle as I lift myself up onto the truck.

"Question," Adrian attempts to pull my attention her way for a moment. "Would you possibly want to work with me at the resale shop?" She quickly explains, "I know your many scholarships will cover books and courses, along with room and board. Everyone could use a little cash, right?"

I look at her with a big grin on my face. "Of course, I will. Just know I planned to do it for free until I need to leave for college in the fall. But since you are offering to pay me, I'll take your money."

SEVEN

You can't purchase any major label clothing without over an hour drive. This is one of the 4,724 reasons I want to escape Athens.

TODAY, Adrian and I are command central at her store while the troops comb neighborhoods for treasures on the curb during free-pickup-days. I gave each team a route to run this morning and again this evening. Adrian knew my planning would be thorough. We plan to organize the store into sections and begin setting out products as we price them.

"Wow! The cleaning crew did an awesome job," I announce.

"Yeah, mom and her friends are a force to be reckoned with while in cleaning mode. They had steam cleaners and wet-vacs running all day."

"It's great that your entire family helps out." I smile as she moves a metal clothes rack to the right side of the store while I stream our local radio station through a Bluetooth speaker.

Being the only child of parents that were only children, the concept of a family supporting each other is foreign to me. I've been alone with my mother since the age of thirteen. I spend most of my time with my friends to avoid the troubles at home.

"While you perfectly arrange the clothes racks where you want them, I'm going to jazz up your front window a bit." I walk through the backroom to my car for the surprise I created for her windows.

Adrian busies herself arranging the clothing section of the store into a children's, teens', women's and men's area as she envisioned. I strategically cover the windows and doors by taping newsprint over them. The thin paper blocks out some but not all of the sunlight. This is good; it will help make the large letters that I've painted on the front of the newspaper pop just a little bit more. I realize Adrian may see letters painted on the paper, but she can't make out the words from the back.

Soon, I approach, waving a blue bandana at her. "Cover your eyes, please."

She shakes her head at me. "I can see the paper. I know there are words on it. Why do I have to cover my eyes?"

"Fine. Let's go out and take a look at my hours of hard work." I tease smiling brightly as I tug her arm towards the backdoor.

Once we make our way around the entire strip mall and down to the front of her store, she seems amazed at my work. She reads out loud, "Coming Soon! Gingham Frog Repurposed Treasures." The words "Gingham" and "Frog" are green and white gingham squares. "Coming Soon" is crimson while "Repurposed Treasure" looks like old boards are nailed together to make the letters. It's not just a sign; it's a work of art.

"I…" She fans her face as she gulps in air. "It's absolutely perfect! Madison, this must have taken you forever to make."

I smile proudly, eyes on the covered storefront. "I had a little help. Winston supplied the newsprint and suggested what to write on it. I mentioned it to Mrs. Foster in art class. She helped me come up with the design to make it pop." I turn to face her, smile still wide.

"I didn't want black letters on paper. It needed to be special, like you."

Adrian wraps me in a tight hug as tears fall from her eyes. "Thank you."

My buzzing phone interrupts our moment. "Better get back inside," I announce. "Troy's group has a full load, and they are almost here."

MY STOMACH GROWLS LOUDLY, demanding I give it attention. I look at my cell phone to find it is nearly seven. "We should think about dinner soon," I tell Adrian. She nods and tells me she will take care of it. I barely blink before she places her cell phone at her ear, on her way to the backroom. I rearrange the rack we are currently working on by size as she retrieves more clothing from the back.

"I texted everyone that pizza will be here in twenty minutes," Adrian informs me, emerging from the backroom with her arms full of children's clothes on hangers. We quickly place them on the front rack.

I step back, admiring the progress we made today. Nearly all of the clothing stock fills several metal racks on the right half of the sales floor. She placed Troy's repurposed furniture on the left side near the large windows for future customers to see. Adrian hopes seeing them in the windows will pull customers inside. Then, she has shelves full of household items and the electronics plugged in at the wall. I love the fact that her customers can ensure they work before purchasing them.

The muted green back wall pops against the stark white side walls. The green adds color to the large, fluorescent-lighted store space.

Adrian opens her Notes App and reads through her pre-opening checklist. She still needs interior and exterior signs, changing rooms, check-out counter, and advertising. She crosses off inventory as we filled much of the space today. She's happy with our progress.

"Pizza guy is out back!" Winston announces from the backroom.

I scurry to meet him, waving at Winston as I pass. He informs Adrian his truck is full of more furniture, some good quality coats, and books.

"Crap!" Adrian shouts. "I forgot to put up shelves for books and vinyl records." She slowly browses the non-clothing side of her store for a space to add shelving.

Placing his hands upon her shoulders, Winston soothes, "Calm down. Let's enjoy our pizza with the gang, and let Latham share an idea he thought of today." Winston smirks. "He's got you covered." With Winston's help, she sets up a folding card table and enough chairs for all of us.

"We're back!" Troy yells.

Adrian smiles widely while Troy, Salem, Latham, Savannah, and Bethany emerge from the backroom as I bring up the rear carrying the pizzas. Our friends have helped Adrian immensely today. She admitted she was a bit worried about filling her sales floor prior to her grand opening but after today, it's full.

"LATHAM," Winston speaks through his current bite of pizza. "Tell Adrian your idea." He winks at her before she turns her attention to Latham.

"Why don't you let us guys build you a horseshoe shaped countertop to use as a check-out area? We can make it two-tiered and even include cabinets below it for storage." Sensing Adrian not following his description, he sketches it out on his napkin. "We also found a large shelving unit we can paint or stain and anchor to the wall for you to display products on."

Latham constantly surprises me. At first glance, he's a farm boy or a cowboy. He's all tall and lanky, wearing western shirts, worn Levi's, dusty boots, and his cowboy hat. Occasionally, he'll wear a solid-colored t-shirt and a John Deere or Dekalb cap. Only close friends know underneath he's really long, lean muscles with a wicked farmers tan. I nearly died of laughter the first time he joined us at the lake. It was as if his legs and chest hadn't seen sunlight his entire life.

The man can fix about anything—it must be from tinkering around his parents' farm on equipment and buildings for years. He's fixed many of our cars, and now he's planning to construct counters and cabinets for her store.

Salem has herself quite a hottie. His jawline usually sports two days of dark stubble. His dark hair, that peeks from under his hat, with dark eyes on his tanned face are like catnip to all the girls. When he smiles, his face and eyes light up all sexy-like, melting the panties off any females in the area. When Adrian states she loves his idea, said sex-smoldering smile shines like a hundred-watt bulb. I may need to remind Adrian he belongs to Salem.

"We could varnish it if you prefer a wood finish or paint it any color you desire," Troy chips in. "I have most of the wood we need, so the cost would be minimal."

"When could you build it?" Adrian inquires, wondering if they can finish it before she opens.

"We can start this weekend," Latham says.

"If we work Friday night and Saturday, we should have it done by Sunday," Troy promises.

Troy is all bulk to Latham's long and lean. Clothes cannot conceal his massive arms and chest. His jeans hug his huge, muscular thighs. If he wasn't nearly six-feet tall, he'd look too heavy. He enjoys working with his hands. Lucky for Adrian, he loves working on furniture and hopes to sell it in her store.

"Really?" She can't believe her ears. "You'd give up your weekend to do this for me?"

"It will cost you meals and drinks," Latham states.

"You've got a deal. I'll give Winston my spare key, so you can get in and out if I'm not around. Will it make much of a mess?"

I sense that Adrian worries her mother's hard day of cleaning might be ruined as well as all the inventory we've already displayed.

"We'll throw sheets over nearby stuff, keep the saws out back, and the mess will be minimized." Adrian smiles at Troy's statement.

Quick and not too messy; I love these guys even more for being Adrian's heroes.

EIGHT

There are no Chinese, Italian, or barbeque places in Athens. This is one of the 4,724 reasons I want to escape this town.

I START my morning in the cemetery, letting the sound of nearby birds fill my excited soul. When I can't hang with friends, I escape to my favorite place. It's a short walk across my neighbor's pasture and the chain link fence keeping livestock from disturbing this area, never stops me from entering. The cemetery where my dad rests requires a drive and is frequented by the citizens of Athens paying their respects. In this long-forgotten cemetery, I often think of my dad, talk to him, and contemplate my future. It also allows me a break from my mother, her drinking, and often hurtful words.

Now, I think about the importance of this day for the families of Athens. For me, it's just a ceremony I must attend. My mother went out until 3:00 a.m. last night—she is in no condition to watch me graduate, not that she planned to.

I'm sure Adrian will be sad that our graduation day has arrived. I need to remember to text her to place tissues in her pockets. She still wants to deny the fact that I will leave Athens for college this fall. Of our tight group of nine, only two aspire to ever leave. Hamilton and I have planned our post-graduation exit for the past four years. College is our excuse, our catalyst to our life beyond Athens. In a twist of fate, we will be attending the same college in the fall.

I chose the education department at The University of Missouri-Columbia fall my junior year after extensively researching available scholarships and work-study programs. I planned to keep my grades up and earn a full-tuition scholarship. Here we are, a year and a half later, my mission accomplished.

Although he excelled in all sports and toyed with the idea of participating in both track and baseball post-high school, Hamilton chose to allow the college baseball scouts choose his launching site. He was heavily scouted for the past two years by Division-1 universities in Texas, Florida, Arizona, Nebraska, Iowa, and Missouri. He narrowed it down to Nebraska, Missouri, and Texas by fall his senior year. After college visits and awards package discussions, he committed to Mizzou with me.

To say I'm excited we will both be Mizzou Tigers is an understatement. One of my best friends will be attending college with me in the fall. I'll already have one friend on campus and someone to hang with. I'll get to attend his games instead of following him online from a distance.

In my new life this fall, I will attend class, go to the store, or go out to eat and not know everything about everyone there. The people I interact with daily will be diverse in the lives they led before college, and their future goals for work and family will vary, unlike those of my friends in Athens. With the exception of Hamilton, no one will know of my alcoholic mother. I won't be judged by her actions or thought to be destined to follow in her footsteps. In Athens, I'm haunted by horrible memories created by my mother in the years since my dad passed. I feel like there's nothing to keep me here. Sure, I will miss my friends, but I want more. I want diversity, culture, adventure, and variety. I want to go out and not know 90% of the people I see. At college this fall, my life will begin.

NINE

Forget six degrees of separation, most locals are only three people away from sharing relatives. I crave variety. Another of the 4,724 reasons I need to leave this town.

ADRIAN SMILES as she walks up to join Hamilton and me on the grass just outside the school. As our group of nine friends arrive, preparing to graduate today, Adrian hasn't hidden her sadness that two of us plan to leave Athens behind. I haven't shared with her that I imagine once I'm in Columbia I will try to avoid visiting Athens like the plague.

Although I often knock the small-town life they crave, I've hidden most of my excitement to leave and my true plans for a life after college. I desire new friends, a new community, and a future far from my mother. This means I also look forward to a new life free of Adrian, Salem, Bethany, and Savannah. I know we will remain in touch for a while via texts and email, but as I don't plan to drive back to Athens, we will drift apart

Hamilton's talent on the baseball diamond will ensure he never moves back to town. I'm his biggest fan and plan never to lose touch with him. He is close to his mom and sister, so he will visit when he can, but he will live and play in a city much larger than Athens, Missouri.

I don't fault Adrian for loving everything about Athens. Unlike me, she is close to both her parents. She's always felt safe and looks forward to raising her future children here. Major crimes and tragedies are rare in this little farm community. I cringe at the small pool of candidates for a future husband that awaits Adrian in this town, but she states they will have known each other most of their lives. She's only minutes away from her family for any support she might need. Unlike me, she can't wait to open her business and raise her family in the town she loves.

My eyes follow Adrian as she approaches a flailing Winston. I smile as he attempts to place his cap on his sandy-blonde hair. After graduation, he will run the family's three-plex movie theater in Athens. Taking over his family's business this summer is all he has talked about recently. Next to him, Troy looks so happy with Bethany in his bulky arms. They will be moving in together in two days. They'll soon start classes at the local community college. Troy plans to become an Athens' Police Officer, and Bethany hopes to teach elementary kids.

At Adrian's side, Latham is very uncomfortable in his black cap and gown. I've never seen him in public without his jeans, boots, or a hat.

"I'm wearing a black dress," Latham pouts. "I'd rather go barefoot than wear these old-man shoes." He lifts one foot in our direction.

"Hey," Winston chides. "They look just like mine."

Latham motions that Winston just proved his point.

Salem attempts to calm him by telling him that he looks very handsome. The sparkle in her eyes for him gives me hope that someday I might find the man of my dreams, too. Latham plans to work his family farm, and Salem will attend community college this summer with dreams of nursing in her future.

Last, but not least, Savannah approaches our group, running a bit late as usual. She mumbles curse words as she fights to put on her cap and gown in the gusty May breeze. No one is really sure what the future holds for Savannah, not even herself. For now, she works at the local grocery store part-time.

"Bring it in," Adrian prompts our friends. With arms over each other's shoulders, we make a circle and lower our heads. In what might look like a rugby scrum to outsiders, she speaks to our tight-knit group. "We've made it! Today we graduate. It's the last step before adulthood. As we walk across the stage today, I want you all to know I couldn't have made it through high school without you. I vow to keep us together as we attempt to spread our wings and move on to bigger and better things in the next couple of months. I love each and every one of you. I will always be here to bail you out of jail, laugh at your stupid mistakes, and kick your ass when you need it." I can hear the lump forming in her throat as she speaks, and I can imagine her eyes beginning to fill up with tears. "I love you. Now let's go get a diploma!"

Cheers erupt as we break apart only to take turns with high-fives and one-armed guy-hugs. Our administrator calls for us to take our places in the line. The ceremony is about to start, and forty-five of us have to be in alphabetical order. We rush off to find our spots.

Bored in the single file line, I dread the impending graduation party. It's just another reminder of how messed up my life is. I feel a bit guilty at my desire to leave such good friends behind. Adrian talked the parents of my eight friends into planning one large joint party for the nine of us. She claims it is to allow us to spend the entire day together, but I know it's really because my mother would not be throwing me a graduation party and Adrian didn't want me to feel left out. Our large party will be at Winston's parents house. Each of us decorated an individual table reflecting on our school years. Hamilton insisted his table sit next to mine, so his mother could stand near both of us. Memphis took me under her wing shortly after Hamilton and I grew close in eighth grade. I know I only survived these last five years because she acted as my surrogate mother. I imagine I will spend the party counting down the hours until we can change into comfortable clothes and party at the bonfire on the sandbar tonight.

TEN

There is a blue-law in Athens, only gas stations, restaurants, and grocery stores may be open on Sunday's. This is one of the 4,724 reasons I want to leave this town.

"I COME BEARING GIFTS," Salem sings as she enters from the backroom.

Adrian and I look up from the laptop. Salem carries a large paper grocery bag in each hand. We already ate lunch and Adrian didn't assign any tasks for her to assist the store with. "What ya got?" Adrian asks, our curiosity peaked.

Salem places the bags on the floor, then bends over out of our view behind the counter the guys made. She emerges, placing a white picture frame glued on a candle holder upon the counter. Our brows furrow as we try to understand her gift. She slowly spins the frame around. "Ta-da!"

The white five-by-seven frame on its stand proudly displays a gingham green paper with very large, bold, black words. The first line reads "Tadpoles" and below it reads, "Children's Clothing". Before I can express my love of this sign, Salem explains they can sit atop the round metal clothing racks on the sales floor.

"They are perfect!" I'm sure Adrian loves that she played with the word "frog" from her store name.

"I have three 'Tadpoles' for the kids' racks, two 'Froglets' signs for the teen's racks, three 'Female Frogs' signs for the women's racks, and two 'Male Frogs' signs for the men's racks." Salem stands tall, pride for her work evident.

"Will you help me put them out?" Adrian allows Salem to place each sign, making them visible from the front of the store. We notice she even alternated the colors from white to green as the frogs grow bigger.

Tears pool as Adrian attempts not to cry. "Thank you," her quivering voice squeaks.

Winston's voice from the back door breaks the moment. "I have a surprise for you," he calls. Taking in the two of them wiping tears and red-faced, he pauses. "I'm sorry. I can come back later…"

"No!" Adrian blurts. "Salem brought me these signs she crafted, and it just brought me to tears."

"We've cried enough," Salem vows. "What's the surprise?"

Winston approaches in his collared shirt and golf shorts. As always, his outfit matches his shoes. I swear he owns more shoes than I do. His sandy-blonde hair, styled with product, is perfect. My fingers always ache to rumple it a bit. No man should ever be so put together. I like guys a bit rougher around the edges. I'm not looking for a bad boy—Winston's golfer style does nothing for me.

He places the heavy box he carries on the front counter. As he fumbles to open the lid to reveal the gifts inside, I can't help wondering why Adrian is receiving so many gifts today.

Winston raises a pale green paper for us to see. It's a flyer. It announces the opening of a new business in Athens, the name of her store, and the items it will include. Details for selling and donating to the store are also printed on the bottom.

"Winston," Adrian searches for the words to express her gratefulness.

"Troy and I plan to run them to businesses all over Athens, hopes they will display them for you." Winston explains his plan. "We will post them on community bulletin boards anywhere we can. We will talk to businesses to ask if they will allow us to leave a stack for customers to take one. Of course, we will display them at my theater."

"I have a few other ideas for you." Winston places a few flyers in a stack on her counter before closing the box. "I'd like to text you when Troy and I are about done so we can eat, and I can share them with you."

Salem elbows Adrian's ribcage. She startles from her thoughts. "I could do dinner tonight." A blush grows on her cheeks.

"It should be about six or so," he informs her as he secures the box of flyers in his arm and strides to the backroom to leave.

"Winston," she calls to him. When he pauses, turning to face Adrian, he smiles. "Thank you." He simply nods, smiling, and leaves.

LATE THAT NIGHT, I'm on the phone with Adrian. She called me, frustrated with all she still needs to do.

"I may never get to sleep tonight. Although I took notes on my phone as Winston and I ate dinner, everything still swirls around, adding questions and items for me to place on my to do list. Don't get me wrong, I'm grateful Winston shares everything he has learned from his parents' business with me. It's just that I've been working so hard doing everything to start my new store, and he just added many more items."

Adrian talks a mile a minute. I try but I can't speak while she continues.

"With his help, I plan to join the Athens Chamber of Commerce, the Athens Jaycees, advertise in the Athens Gazette, and on our local radio station." Adrian quickly lists these items, further demonstrating the stress she's under. "He pointed out how each will help my business. I hope it will not be too overwhelming. He promises he will attend the meetings and events with me. He's been attending with his parents, so he can introduce me to community members that can help my business, too. I don't understand why he is taking such an interest in helping me with my business, but I am glad he is."

Finally finding a break in her words, I begin. "Friends help friends. Winston enjoys helping you. I can see it on his face. I think he's glad he's not the only one of our group choosing business over college. The two of you have that in common."

Adrian tilts her head to the side, contemplating my words for a moment, before we finally say goodnight. I smile. Hamilton once told me, a drunk Winston confessed to him Adrian was hot. Winston hasn't acted on it, but I can see he still likes her.

ELEVEN

Athens doesn't even have a Walmart—it's another of the 4,724 reasons I want to escape this town.

I'VE NEEDED to pee for two hours now. I refuse to leave Adrian alone on her first day open. Her parents are here now, so I finally have a chance to excuse myself to the backroom.

My feet ache from standing all day. I should have thought better of my flip-flops on the concrete floor. I will know for tomorrow. I take a few sips of a diet-cola from the fridge before stepping back on the sales floor. I'm exhausted but love every minute of it.

I position myself at the pay station for the remainder of the day as Adrian and her parents work the floor. I begin making a list of items we need to restock from the backroom before we open tomorrow. We have a few furniture pieces in back but will need Troy to bring more as soon as possible.

Adrian's mother locks the front door at six, her father begins moving furniture for us, Adrian stocks the clothes, and I run the end of day sales receipts and count the cash. I leave start up cash in the drawer and prepare the rest for deposit.

"Your attention please," I call to the room. "Our opening day total is $479.54."

"Nearly $500," Winston cheers entering from the back, startling all of us. "What a busy day you've had." His big, blue eyes are clearly locked on Adrian as he approaches. "Congratulations, Adrian." He places a chaste kiss on her cheek.

Adrian nervously thanks him, stating that she never could have done this without his help.

"Well, I really couldn't have done it without all of her help." She corrects sweeping her hand around the room.

Winston and Adrian's father return to moving furniture, and Adrian finds a spot at the clothing racks next to me, pretending to look busy.

I catch her sideways glances in Winston's direction. I witness the small smile she tries to hide while I assume, she's thinking of him. She has it bad, and she's doing everything she can to deny it, which is odd. Adrian rarely holds back—when she wants something she goes for it. She's interested in Winston, but she's hesitating. The cat-and-mouse game they are playing is very entertaining.

I elbow her. "Are you okay? It's been a big day. You should take the deposit and go home. I'll lock up for you." I know there is no way she will leave before me.

We make quick work of closing up. Winston insists on escorting Adrian to the bank with the deposit. Since I did the end of day receipts, I know most of her income today is credit cards—I don't believe $100 requires an escort for safety. It's cute how Winston is weaving himself into her life.

TODAY IS GAME DAY. Baseball season is my favorite time of the year. I love the smell of fresh cut grass, the heat of the sun, and the taste of sunflower seeds. Nothing beats the view from the top of the bleachers during the National Anthem as the two teams stand near the fresh chalk lines to address the Stars and Stripes.

I love the rituals each team and player believe in. Hamilton is one of the most superstitious players I've ever known. His mom delivers a cold Snickers bar to him in the dugout before each game. He has rules for hanging his uniform, each one specific. First on the hanger, his socks and his belt. Next, his pants. His sleeves go on next, then the jersey. Lastly, his hat slips over the bend of the hook. He always loads his bat-bag and sleeps with his glove under his pillow the night before a game. Each year, he writes The Lord's Prayer on the underside of the bill of his cap with an ink pen so it's visible to his eyes only during the game. He winks at his mom and me in the on-deck circle before each at bat. In the event of a team loss he refuses to wash his socks until they win again. Fortunately, the Blue Jays win most of the time.

I hardly slept a wink last night. I fear I am more anxious about today's home opener than Hamilton is. I attempt to busy myself cleaning my room, doing laundry, and washing my car to pass the time this morning. I still have two hours before the first pitch. I decide to head into Athens. Maybe I will find someone to visit with until it's time to show up at the field.

Upon entering town, I need to stop at the grocery store to procure snacks for the double-header today. I grab a hand-held basket to carry as I shop. I choose one box of Milk Duds to consume before they melt, a Mike & Ike box, Dakota Sunflower Seeds, and Tootsie Pops. Every game, I bring the same four items. I always bring my own —I can't take the risk the concession stand is out or doesn't carry them.

I'm as superstitious as Hamilton is. He has his game day routines, and I have mine. I don't have to consume all four items, but they must be in my possession at the game. It's a team effort, and I do my part.

I wear my replica jersey, although I have created two new shirts to wear to games this season. I refuse to break them in at a game in which Hamilton will be the starting pitcher. I can't risk bad luck on behalf of my new shirt.

Before I pull out from the grocery parking lot, I text Adrian, Savannah, Bethany, and Salem.

Me: I'm early, anyone ready for the game?
Adrian: Pick me up, I'm ready.
Me: heading your way now
Salem: I'll be there soon
Salem: Savannah gets off at game time.
Me: See ya soon

WITH MY SNACKS and cooler of water in hand, Adrian and I head across the parking lot toward the ball park. Adrian carries her homemade, blue, white, and red colors, fleece blanket for us to sit on in the wooden bleachers. As we approach, the team is warming up in the outfield, Hamilton is throwing in the bullpen, and a few parents from both teams sit in lawn chairs scattered around the infield fence. Adrian and I sit on the top row of the bleachers in our usual corner.

As game time draws near, I don't see Hamilton's mother here yet—this concerns me. From the height of our seats, I search the parking lot, but her truck is not there. I purchase a Snickers bar at the concession stand before making my way to the home team dugout. Through the gaps between wooden boards, I spot Hamilton on the end of the bench. Without a word, I pass the candy bar through a crack. Hamilton grabs it with a smile. In his mother's absence, I couldn't let this pregame ritual go undone. I only hope he doesn't worry why his mother is not here. As his head coach doesn't allow girls near the players on gameday, I quietly slip back to my seat in the stands. My cell phone vibrates in my pocket.

Hamilton: TY, mom told me she'd be here @ game time today

SHOCKED that he is using his cell phone as they are prohibited in the dugout, I look toward the field and note both coaches are speaking to the umpires near home plate. With no coach in the dugout, Hamilton took a second to message me. I hurry to reply so he doesn't get caught.

Me: No worries, Good Luck

TWELVE

Everyone waves at everyone while driving. Yet another of the 4,724 reasons I want to escape Athens.

THE SATURDAY after Adrian's store opens, Troy and Bethany wed in a private ceremony at the courthouse before their parents host a reception party. Our group of friends volunteered to assist the parents with decorating the stone building on the fairgrounds for the reception. Salem gathered props and is currently setting up a photo booth area near the front door. Savannah and Adrian string fairy lights from the rafters.

Troy's parents place centerpieces on each table. Troy's mother crafted a simple floral piece, then added handcuffs and ABC chalkboards along with other cop and teacher paraphernalia.

Bethany's mother harasses the caterer as she sets up the wedding cake table. Her father conveniently is nowhere to be found. I assist Latham and Hamilton as they set up the DJ table. The guys will play music from our playlists, saving the parents money. As

Savannah and Adrian climb down the ladders to plug in the last strand, I approach.

"Wow, this looks amazing." After several moments, we pull our eyes from the twinkle lights. "Wanna help me request a few songs to start the evening?" I wave an ink pen and clipboard towards them. We giggle as we jot down a couple of our favorite songs.

Salem's raised voice interrupts our brainstorming session. "Ladies, I can't find Bethany's father anywhere. Someone needs to pull her mom away to rescue the poor caterer." We follow Salem's extended arm pointing toward the cake table. "I'm worried the caterer might burst into tears soon."

Adrian accepts the challenge and distracts Mrs. Lamar by asking her to let us know if we need to adjust any light strings. While they walk the entire space, analyzing light spacing, I notice the caterer dash away from the barn.

"Special delivery!" Mr. Lamar shouts as he rolls a cart of beverages toward the refreshment tables.

The four of us assist him in displaying the various drinks, cups, and ice along with the snack mix, nuts, and popcorn.

"Perfect," Troy's mother announces. "It's time we all go cleanup. Remember to be back here by 6 p.m."

WALKING ON THE FAIRGROUNDS, I marvel at how this large, stone barn, built in 1938, transforms into a charming venue. The rustic stone facade loses its golden hues for a shaded gray as the summer sun begins to set. The warm stones embody strength to stand many storms in years to come just as I believe Troy and Bethany's union will stand the test of time.

Adrian wraps her arms around Savannah and me. "Can you believe we are adults? I mean, we are 18, and our friends are now married. I know adulting will not be easy, but with friends like you, I will survive." She places a kiss on both our cheeks before throwing open the heavy doors. Turning to face us, she asks, "Who's ready to party?"

The three of us freeze just inside the front doors. Bethany and Troy's parents occupy a table at the far side of the barn. The fairy lights shine from above, and the large space is completely silent.

"This will not do." Adrian strides to the music table.

I quickly turn on the five Bluetooth speakers strategically placed around the dance area and near the doors. Adrian selects Latham's country music playlist to entertain us. Keith Urban's lyrics fill the space as two of Troy's relatives enter. Savannah places their gift on the gift table before Salem whisks them into the photo booth.

Adrian and I greet a steady influx of guests while Savannah and Salem continue to man their stations over the next hour. Promptly at 7 p.m., Troy escorts our beautiful Bethany into the party amidst cheers. Fair-complected Bethany flushes red head to toe while both hands cover her mouth.

I love her reaction to our decorations, her family, and friends.

"Ladies and gentlemen, Mr. and Mrs. Troy Sullivan," Latham's voice announces into the microphone.

Troy attacks Bethany's mouth with a hot, somewhat inappropriate kiss for such a public venue. Loud cheers fill the space. The couple slowly greets each guest, working their way through the room.

I join the rest of our gang at the music table where Salem attempts to persuade the group toward the photo booth. Adrian quickly joins in her persuasive endeavor. I fetch the dry erase props and a marker.

On one large arrow I write "most likely to wear plaid at his wedding" and points, it at Latham. While we laugh, I write "most likely to marry a Barbie Doll", pointing it at Hamilton.

I erase both signs. "What would you write on mine?" I taunt the guys as I slowly back up towards the photo area. The guys accept my challenge and follow.

Adrian suggests Hamilton and I go first. The rest of the group giggle as they conspire to write on our dry erase arrows. They don't allow us to see the words as we hold the signs and a picture is snapped. Hamilton's sign states "most likely to earn millions". My sign reads "most likely to become famous". After the photo and reading each sign, we argue their choice of words. As a future teacher, I claim fame seems like a huge stretch. I remind them that Hamilton will be famous for his baseball career. Hamilton begins to argue, but I shut him up with the raising of one hand in front of his face".

We continue taking turns with groups of two, four, and all seven of us. Bethany and Troy join us for two photos of our group of nine. Troy writes "most likely to share a jail cell together" for one of our pictures.

I excuse myself to answer my cell phone when it vibrates. I can't imagine who might be calling as our group of friends are all at this party. As I walk away, Latham informs the group the display showed unknown caller.

THIRTEEN

I'll never escape the judgement that I am just like my mother; yet another of the 4,724 reasons I want to escape this town.

"HELLO. THIS IS MADISON." I greet the unknown caller interrupting Troy and Bethany's reception.

"Ms. Crocker, I'm Officer Campbell at the Athens Police Station. Your mother was brought in for driving under the influence and resisting arrest..."

As his voice continues in my ear, I don't hear a word he says. She's done it again. This is her second DUI. I cringe at the possibility she might have hurt others with her decision to drive impaired. I've attempted to help her attend Alcoholics Anonymous. I've urged her to speak to our minister and others. I've pleaded with her to call me for a ride. My words fell on deaf ears. I thank the officer for calling then hang-up.

Turning around, I find Troy standing in my path to return to the party. He heard me thanking Officer Campbell. Troy's very close to the officers as he hopes to become one.

"Your mom at the station?"

I can only nod while attempting to hold back my anger and tears.

"Let's go."

I blink up at Troy attempting to understand his words. Shaking my head, I find my voice. "Troy, you can't leave your reception. You need to get back inside to Bethany." I gently push his chest. "I'll join you in a few more minutes."

I lean against a wooden pole in the livestock barn. During the fair this area is alive with animals, farmers, and youth. Now it's quiet and free of the smells associated with livestock. I don't know what to do to help my mom. I can't make her second DUI go away. Maybe this time she will wake up to the risky behavior she's engaging in.

A large, warm hand connects with my lower back. "Troy asked me to accompany you to the police station." Hamilton positions himself in front of me. "My truck is over here."

Without thinking my body moves alongside his. He opens the passenger door then holds my hand as I carefully climb into the cab in my dress. I look his way when he turns the key in the ignition and the engine roars to life.

"She'll be okay." His words mean to comfort me. I simply nod, though I'm not feeling confident.

At the station, Hamilton maintains constant contact with me to show his support. I do feel stronger with his hand in mine, on my lower back, and on my shoulder. We learn my mother will be kept overnight to sleep off her bender. They divulge the location of her car, hand me the keys, and encourage me to return after 10 a.m. to pick mom up.

Hamilton and I slip back into the reception. While he fetches beverages, I join our friends at the table. Adrian embraces me before I can sit. No words are spoken.

Hamilton places our two drinks on the table. "Why aren't people dancing?"

All heads turn to the dance floor. It seems my friends were too worried about me to keep the party atmosphere lively. To ensure Troy and Bethany's reception remains magical, we rise and start dancing as I attempt to ignore my mother's mess.

BETHANY GRASPS my hand and proceeds to tug me from the dance floor. She is a woman on a mission as she leads me outside. As the door closes the music fades and we find ourselves surrounded by the dark summer night.

"Troy shared about your mother." I avert my eyes unable to witness the pity on her face. "I must confess I've wanted to share something with you but worried you might think I was overstepping." She takes both my hands in hers. "My father is in AA." She watches my face as her words sink in. "He's now sober seven years. It wasn't pretty when he hit rock-bottom. I want to share this because I know what you are going through. I could speak to my dad and see if he might talk to your mom. By sharing his journey, it might help her."

"I don't know. I've mentioned Alcoholics Anonymous several times. It seems to upset her causing her to drink more."

"Why don't you think about it. I'm not going anywhere—my offer still stands." She releases my hands, placing them on my shoulders while looking me straight in the eyes. "I found virtual Al-Anon and Alateen meetings. Since Athens doesn't have a group here, I used the internet to connect with others in similar situations. I found it helped chatting with others." She pauses deepening her stare. "Go to Al-Anon's website and join a virtual meeting. It helps. You've endured this too long on your own, it's time to reach out."

I nod. Bethany hugs me before announcing it's time we return to the party. No longer in the party mood, I will fake it for my friends on their special day.

FOURTEEN

When a house catches on fire, the adults all call each other to gossip about it. This is one of the 4,724 reasons I want to escape this town.

ADRIAN TOTALLY IGNORES my insistence that I can handle picking my mother up at the police station by myself. She hid my car keys last night for fear I might attempt to leave while she slept. Shaking the keys in front of me, she states she is accompanying me to the police station and taking my mother home.

Pulling into the lot at the police station, Adrian growls, "I can't believe they texted Troy."

"You've got to be kidding me." Adrian scowls, "Boys can be so dumb. I can't believe they texted Troy while he was on his honeymoon."

"Adrian." My tone conveying that I'm upset the entire gang is here, "I don't need an audience today. It's embarrassing enough without the entire town of Athens talking about it."

Trying to lighten the mood, she reminds me the gossips of Athens heard about the DUI on their police scanners last night. I sigh. Adrian reminds me they are here for me, I can't drive both cars home, and I might need them to assist with my mother. She explains she didn't know if my mother would be mean to me and couldn't bear the thought of me physically attempting to get my mother home. That's why she texted for the muscles to join us. Resigning to the current situation, I open my car door.

Troy approaches, stopping us in our tracks. "Madison, she's pissed off. I spoke to the desk clerk. You need to sign a form, then they will release her to you." Troy looks to Adrian for support before continuing. "I could hear her ranting while I was at the front desk. She's already mad at you and not using flattering words when referring to you. I want you to be ready for it. This will not be fun. But we are all here to help. Please understand we know she doesn't mean anything she is about to say to you."

I nod, sigh deeply, then with head high and shoulders back I stride into the station. Minutes later, I open the door and peek my head out. I ask Troy and Hamilton to help. The two men carry my mother from the station to the backseat of the car with her shrieking the entire way.

"You whore." I no longer flinch when the drunken words pierce my heart. "Had to beg your boyfriends to drag your mom home today, didn't you?" The guys struggle against her attempts to slap as they close the car door. Only slightly muffled she continues her screaming through the car window. "She misses her daddy, I bet she gives you every dirty thing you ask for just to keep you from leaving her." I mouth the words "I'm sorry," to Troy and Hamilton while I attempt to fight the sting of tears threatening the back of my eyes. "Pathetic slut. She'll do anything to prevent being alone with me."

My mother is only partially right. It's not my daddy issues, but her drunken stupors that cause me to seek the company of my friends. I miss my dad, but I am not sexually active due to daddy issues. She's projecting. She's the one seeking men to erase the pain of losing my dad.

My mother's words are hard for me to ignore. I'm not sure how my friends can ignore the hateful taunts. I've shared how mean my drunk mother was with Adrian. She isn't drunk now. She pretends she can't even find the strength to walk, yet she can belittle me, her only living relative, publicly. This is why I'm counting the days until I can escape to college.

Luckily, my mother falls asleep as we drive through Athens. Thankful for the silent passenger in the backseat, I don't dare whisper to wake her. I grasp Adrian's hand in mine, giving her a tight squeeze of thanks.

Hamilton's red truck sits in the driveway when Adrian places the car in park. Troy and Latham pull up behind us in my mother's car. The guys gather outside the backseat door and plan. Adrian and I hold the doors open while the men carry my still sleeping mother into the house. I cringe as they near her bedroom.

My friends attempt to control their reactions to their surroundings. I've allowed Adrian inside our house once many years ago. Hamilton entered a time or two, also long ago. Mother's bedroom is decorated in recycled chic; empty vodka and whiskey bottles adorn every surface and the floor. I cringe at the large wastebasket full of bottles near the door. We must tread carefully during our exit to refrain from kicking a bottle. The last thing we want is to wake her.

Back outside, I assure everyone my mother will sleep all day. I encourage them to leave, promising I'll come to dinner and the movies with them tonight. Hamilton clearly wishes to remain with me, but Troy, Latham, and Adrian need him to give them a lift to town. They say their goodbyes while making me promise to call if I need them or want to talk.

I'm sure they discuss my situation on the fifteen-minute drive to Athens. My mother wasn't always like this. We were the perfect family while my dad was alive. We camped, cooked, and were in public together. I was close to both parents. It's hard to see my mother now and remember how normal she was years ago.

I believe my mother's heart broke with my father's death. I think she drinks to forget the love she lost and believes she'll never find again. She's the only family I've got and she doesn't make it easy to be around her.

FIFTEEN

Everyone knows everything about everyone—this is another of the 4,724 reasons I want to escape Athens.

LATE IN THE AFTERNOON, I quickly grab my vibrating phone. I am walking on eggshells trying not to wake my mother.

Bethany: Ready for dinner & movie?
Me: Yes
Bethany: Good. I'm in your driveway

WHAT? *She's here? Why would she drive all the way out to my house?* I grab my cash and quietly slip from the house.

Bethany waves through her open car window. She wears her usual smile, but I know she is up to something.

"I'm driving. Hop in."

I slide into her passenger seat and buckle my safety belt.

After she pulls from my driveway, she dives right in. "I don't like to talk about friends when they aren't present. I need to let you know Adrian and Hamilton shared with Troy their memories of your family story before and after your dad's death. Of course, Troy then mentioned it to me and I had an epiphany." Bethany's eyes remain on the road.

I open my mouth to stop her.

"Just hear me out," she continues. "You don't go on many dates. You try to plan group outings instead of alone time with interested guys. You never go out with a guy more than a couple of times. I think you are avoiding the possibility of finding love."

I'm sure my eyes bug out. Is she really going to force a therapy session upon me for the fifteen minutes she has me held captive in her moving car?

"Whether you are aware of it or not, you are afraid. You are trying to prevent the heartache your mother endures."

"You're hurting yourself. Madison, you need to allow yourself the possibility to find love. You can't let your fear of heartache prevent you from experiencing the magic. It breaks my heart."

I argue. "There's no one for me in Athens. I'm waiting for college."

Bethany doesn't believe my lame excuse. "I don't want you to live your entire life never feeling what I have with Troy. You're a terrific friend. You're so caring and genuine. You need to open yourself up to the possibility and let a guy in. Trust me, the joy of love far outweighs the difficult times when you break up with a guy."

I can only smile at Bethany. Her words hit their mark. She's given me much to think about.

SIXTEEN

There are only three movies to choose from with only two showtimes. Reason number 4,724 that I want to escape Athens.

A WEEK LATER, my day starts as any other summer day. I wake, removing my eye mask at about nine. As I tiptoe down the hallway, I peek into her room to find my mother and a couple of empty bottles sprawled on her bed. I hurry to get myself around and leave before she might stir and force me to have to interact with her.

Yesterday, I felt an anxious pit building in my stomach. I thought the big event might happen; of course, Hamilton denies he stands any chance of being drafted at all. Yesterday came and went without a word. I know in my heart it will be today; he deserves to be drafted before the final day.

I climb into the driver's seat at 10:30 a.m. I shoot a quick text to Hamilton's mother prior to starting my car.

Me: I hope you are ready for this
Me: Today will be the day!
Memphis: I love your faith sweetheart
Memphis: but it might not happen at all
Me: I'm headed to your house now
Me: It will be today. Trust me

MY ENGINE GRINDS TO LIFE, and I pull from my driveway. It is a quick drive to Hamilton's family farm. I am proud of the fact I stayed away yesterday, although every part of me wanted to be present when he got a call. I can't stay away anymore. I've been crabby and jumpy since the start of the draft. Today, I can't sit still. I need to be with Hamilton, so I might calm down.

I wave to Hamilton who's working on the tractor near the barn as I walk into his house. Memphis is busy cutting homemade noodles on the kitchen table when I enter.

"Good morning," I sing as I squeeze her from the side quickly and pour myself a glass of iced tea. "Who are all those noodles for?"

She makes quick work of cutting row after row of noodles as flour dusts the air. "Tonight's the Bible study potluck. You know how they love my beef and noodles," she brags, shrugging her shoulders.

"Potluck means everyone brings food. Won't that be way too much?"

"Four of us signed up for the main dish. Everyone else brings salads, sides, or desserts." She wipes her flour-covered hands on her navy apron, leaving white powder everywhere. "There are eighteen of us plus spouses and kids."

"Wow, that will be a large group then." I now understand the need for several batches of noodles. It amazes me she insists on making them from scratch instead of buying them at the store. But, having enjoyed her beef and noodles in the past, I know they taste divine the way she makes them. They are full of love from this magnificent woman.

"Ham is at the barn, tinkering around." Memphis moves from the noodles to the broth simmering in two large roasters on the counter. As she stirs, I notice the beef is already in the broth.

"I waved at him. Anything I can do to help you?" I know I am not a great cook, but with her watching over me, I can't ruin anything.

"You can scoop up handfuls of noodles, and I'll stir as you drop them in." She smiles gratefully. I quickly wash my hands at the sink before I assist moving noodles from the table to the roaster at her prompting.

I love helping Memphis in the kitchen. It reminds me of helping my mom bake before dad arrived home from work each night. In those days, I loved spending time with my mother. She would turn on the radio, and we would sing or dance around the kitchen. Dad liked to make a big production when eating the meals, he knew I assisted with.

"Look at you," Memphis' words draw me from my happy memories. "You've got flour in your hair, on your nose, and all the way up to your elbows." We laugh at my mess. I have no idea how it happened.

"What's going on in here?" Hamilton's deep voice booms from the backdoor. When he enters the kitchen, a smile glides upon his face. It reaches up to the crinkles at the corners of his twinkling brown eyes. "Are we having a flour fight?" he asks, preparing to grab a glob from the table.

"No," his mother warns in that tone that means she is serious. "Madison is just a messy chef." I'm not insulted by her explanation. I know Memphis means it as a compliment.

"I've got the tractor up and runnin' again." Hamilton takes a long drink of my iced tea. "I need to load a few bales of hay and drop 'em off at the Ag building. I promised him I'd be there before lunch. I'm running late. Need anything from town while I am out?" He looks from me to his mother.

"Memphis, why don't we ride along with him and keep him

company?" I suggest. I'm not sure how long his trip to town might take, and I want Memphis present when this important phone call comes today.

Memphis smiles a knowing smile at me. I might be fooling Hamilton today since he is in denial, but nothing gets by her. "Let's stop somewhere for lunch before we head back."

Hamilton excuses himself to clean up. Memphis hands me a wet dishcloth to do the same. She pats the flour from my hair while I take care of my nose and arms.

SEVENTEEN

The radio station airs local high school sporting events and live radar reports during storms, interrupting music for hours. This is one of the 4,724 reasons I want to leave this town.

I QUICKLY GLANCE at my phone and note it is nearly two o'clock as we finish up our meal. In my mind, I know it is day two of the draft. It started at noon today, our time with round three. My nerves kick into high gear as I realize his call might come at any moment.

"Can I drive us back?" I ask Hamilton as I follow him to the driver's door.

He tilts his head to the side and furrows his brow. "Why?"

"My stomach feels a little off from eating lunch so late. I don't want to get carsick," I lie. It's a half-truth. My stomach is in all kinds of knots but not for the reason I gave him. I climb behind the wheel as Hamilton climbs in the passenger side after his mother.

Memphis grins at Hamilton "If you don't have plans this evening you should bring Madison to the potluck dinner."

Being the nice boy, he is, Hamilton promises his mother. "I'll think about it." He throws a smile my way.

When Hamilton's cell phone ringtone blares in the cab, I squeal while attempting to keep the large truck on the road. This is it—I know it. Goosebumps appear over my entire body as the hairs on the back of my neck stand on end. I slow a bit, turn on my blinker and take the next gravel road off the main highway, while Hamilton answers the unknown number.

He looks to me, questioning my actions as he responds to the caller. "Yes, this is Hamilton Armstrong."

I keep the truck running and air conditioner on low but turn off the stereo. My mouth is as dry as a desert. My stomach is full of massive butterflies. I am so excited for my best friend.

"Yes, sir," Hamilton says into his cell. "I'm honored, sir. Might I have a minute to speak with my mother?" He places his phone on mute holding it out from his body.

"Hamilton, what's wrong?" Memphis places her hand on his tanned forearm.

He motions for us to exit the truck. When the three of us stand in front of his truck, he speaks. "Nothing is wrong, Mom." He pauses to look at me then back to Memphis. "It's a member of the Chicago Cubs. Seems they just picked me in the draft today."

Tears and audible sobs escape from a smiling Memphis. Hamilton wraps his long, masculine arms around her. He looks my way while cuddling her. "Get over here, you." I join in this family hug. "What should I tell them?" he teases.

I swat his chest at the same time as Memphis. "You tell them yes," she states, wiping away her tears and fanning her face.

Hamilton takes his phone off mute and continues to talk with the representative. He doesn't speak much, just replies "yes" every now and then.

I pull up a contact on my phone and show it to Hamilton while he listens on his phone.

"Yes, sir, I have his information right here." He rattles off the name of his agent and the digits in his number from my phone screen.

This causes me to beam even more. I insisted he find an agent for when he was drafted. Hamilton stated that would be a few years away. So, I found him an agent that agreed to step in immediately should he be drafted this year. When I close the contact information, I wish I had a better phone so I could open the draft information on the internet.

I quietly ask Memphis if I might borrow her smartphone. Standing next to her with her arm squeezing me, I pull up Draft Tracker. I enlarge it a bit then share it with her. Hamilton was the first pick in the eighth round. Officially, he was pick number two-hundred twenty-five in the draft, selected by the Chicago Cubs as a left-handed pitcher from Athens High School in Athens, Missouri."

Pride swells in my chest. My cheeks begin to ache from smiling so big.

Memphis asks me how I knew. How did I know to encourage him to enter this draft and not wait three years? How did I know today would be the day? And how did I know to drive so he could take the call on our way home?

I shrug before answering. "He's very talented. I've known this for years. I listened in the stands as the college scouts looked at him last summer. That's why I pushed him to enter the draft. He's a left-handed pitcher that throws in the high ninety-two to ninety-five miles per hour range, can play outfield, and can hit. He's a unicorn. He's just what the National League dreams of. Because we are from a small town in Missouri, and he's considered a high school senior in the draft, I figured he'd go somewhere between the fifth and tenth rounds. His stats are enough to make them drool, even if no one in an organization has seen him in action."

I smile proudly. Finally, others see the talent I've marveled at for years.

"It started at noon today, so I figured they were in round five or later by now. I had faith in his talent and faith that a team would see what I see in him." It's hard to explain. It was a feeling based on years of stats, watching him play, watching Major League Baseball on television, and listening to the scouts at his games. He throws very hard for a lefty, and he is only eighteen. With knowledgeable coaching and trainers, he might hit one-hundred miles per hour. I just knew he couldn't be ignored.

Memphis wraps me in a tight hug. "His dream and his father's dream just came true." She kisses my forehead. "He'll leave soon; are we ready for this?" she whispers.

"We've got each other," I remind her. "We will get through this together." Until this moment, the gravity of the situation hadn't fully hit me. Hamilton's plans may change. Our plans may change.

"They are calling my agent right now. We need to hurry home, so I am ready when he calls me. So, let's head that way while I share what I know so far."

I pull back onto the highway as Hamilton shares he has been drafted by the Chicago Cubs Organization. They will now contact his agent to negotiate the terms before they can share the details of when and where this will take him.

That's it. Until he hears from the agent, that's all he knows. Memphis talks excitedly about how proud she is, how proud his father would be, and how much his life might change because he was drafted. I focus only on the road. I can't freak out about a change in our plans until I know for sure.

HAMILTON'S PHONE rings the minute we enter the house. He answers while pulling out a kitchen chair. I pour three tall glasses of tea before joining the two of them at the table.

"I'm putting you on speaker phone," Hamilton announces then presses a button on his iPhone screen. "I'm here with my mother, Memphis, and my best friend, Madison."

"Hello. My name is Nelson Sheridan. Madison, I believe we

spoke on the phone previously." His deep voice is pleasant yet professional.

"Yes, it's a pleasure to speak to you again," I reply as I busy myself opening a nearby notepad and grabbing a pen to take notes for Hamilton.

"I've spoken with the general manager of The Chicago Cubs. I believe we have negotiated terms you will be pleased with, Hamilton." Nelson pauses before continuing. "They are offering a signing bonus of $175,000. This figure is on the high end of those available in the eighth round of the draft this year. The terms of the contract are for you to report to triple-A ball for the remainder of the season in Des Moines, Iowa."

I continue jotting notes as he lists the amount Hamilton will earn for the rest of this year and in subsequent years in the AAA league. I list the figures if he drops to AA or A teams as my head spins. The signing bonus alone has me feeling nauseous. As a future teacher, it is much more than I will make in many years of teaching.

"The terms of the contract lay out contingencies if you are called up to the Majors, but I got them to agree to insert a clause for us to renegotiate prior to that occurring." Nelson sounds proud of this fact. "Our hopes are for you to move up this season or the next. I want to renegotiate after they personally see what a value you will be for their club. I'm confident we will agree on a much larger figure when this occurs, thus the reason for the clause."

Hamilton thanks Nelson for taking care of that.

"Is there anything you want to see in the contract before we verbally agree upon it? Anything you want changed?"

Hamilton finishes a sip of iced tea. "I would like to see the contract state that the club will furnish an apartment or condo for me while I am in the AAA and Major Leagues. Should I drop lower, it will be my responsibility. This will take the burden of searching on my own off my plate, so I may focus solely on the game. I'd also like them to pay for a bachelor's degree either online or in the off-season. Are these possibilities?"

Nelson responds these are very good stipulations and we should further add they supply accommodations in the spring-training city for the off-season also. The two discuss further and end the call with a promise that Nelson will call back after he discusses this with the Cubs.

The three of us sit a moment in silence, staring at each other and sipping our tea.

Memphis is the first to break the silence. "In my wildest dreams, I had no idea the figures were so large."

"What have I been saying forever?" I break in. "Hamilton is a rare unicorn in the MLB. He's a hard throwing lefty that can hit and play the field. He is versatile. He deserves big figures. He will earn even bigger ones."

Hamilton smiles while shaking his head at me. "My number one fan. You've had this figured out for years, haven't you?"

Agreeing, Memphis shares. "I must admit, your texts this morning made me a little nervous, but I still denied it would happen."

Hamilton's brows pinch at Memphis' words. "What text this morning?" He turns to face me.

I explain the texts I sent his mother before I drove over here today. Hamilton's face goes blank.

"You knew it would happen today? You texted my mom that today was the day? That's why you came over, isn't it?" I see the disbelief as he works it all out in his mind. "That's the real reason you wanted to drive my truck home?" He smirks.

I nod. "It was a hunch, a gut feeling. I've believed it for so long, I just knew it would happen."

Hamilton shakes his head, unable to believe I saw this coming. He's still in denial of the magnitude of his abilities. If he ever grasps the enormity of it all, I will pity anyone at the plate to face him.

His cell phone rings. "I've got you on speaker again." Hamilton greets.

"Hello everyone," Nelson greets. "They agreed to all of our

terms. Congratulations, Hamilton, you have a verbal agreement with the Chicago Cubs."

We cheer loudly on our end as Nelson can be heard laughing on the other end of the phone. When our celebration tapers off, Nelson continues. "Someone from the Cubs organization will contact you later today with arrangements for your arrival in Des Moines in two days. Until then, celebrate. You deserve it. And Hamilton, remember to call me if you have any questions anytime day or night."

While Memphis and Hamilton celebrate, I contemplate the fact he will leave us in two days. Hamilton and I are not going to college together this fall. He will leave in two days, and I will finish the summer without him. I end my train of thought right there. Today, I celebrate with my friend and his mom. Tonight, I can allow myself to mourn the plans we shared.

EIGHTEEN

The young cops party with high school kids while off-duty on the weekends, another one of the 4,724 reasons I want to escape this town.

Me: I'm bored, are you coming to town?
Hamilton: About ready to leave
Hamilton: meet you in 20
Me: C Ya Soon

I EXIT my car to sit on the hood. I watch my fellow teenagers of this small burg cruise the strip. August can't arrive soon enough. The only entertainment for the under-twenty-one crowd is Winston's three-plex Theater, to cruise the strip for hours, or to party in remote locations. I choose to busy myself on my cell phone instead of wave at the cruisers.

It's already 8:30 p.m. Hamilton leaves at noon tomorrow for Des

Moines. We planned to attend college together for the next four years; instead, I now have hours before I lose my friend. I'm proud of him, excited he received this opportunity, but I am not ready for hundreds of miles to separate us. Our plan has always been to escape this town together before he played professional baseball. Now we will be leaving Athens in two different directions.

Adrian backs her old truck next to me, lays down the tailgate, and invites me over to sit with her.

"Town's dead tonight," I state.

Adrian offers me a sip of her cup from the local gas station. I shake my head. I don't consume alcohol if I will be driving. "There's a huge party under the bridge tonight. Rumor has it they have two kegs." She grins.

I'm not privy to the party invites. It's not that I am not welcome; it's that I have an alcoholic mother and tend not to drink at such parties. I usually tag along with my friends, attempt to keep everyone safe, and chauffeur several home later. I have fun mingling and watching everyone.

"Want to ride out with us?" Adrian offers, still sipping on her vodka-laced fountain drink.

"Hamilton's on his way in. I'll ride with him." I plan to be stuck to him like glue until noon tomorrow. I have plans for our last night together.

"Speak of the devil..." Adrian laughs as Hamilton pulls his large red truck into the lot.

Finally! It felt like he might never get here! I've thought of nothing all day but my time tonight with Hamilton. He joins us on the tailgate.

"Your last night in Athens," Adrian greets. "I figured you would be out with the guys."

"We hung out last night and today." Hamilton looks to me. "I promised to spend tonight with Madison." Wearing a smirk, I see sparks in his eyes. I guess being drafted by the Chicago Cubs can do that to an eighteen-year-old.

IT'S a normal sandbar party by the river bridge. A large bonfire blazes near the center of the sand. There are several trucks backed in, circling the fire. As we approach, Hamilton is greeted with fist-bumps, high-fives, and words of congratulations. Most offer him beer and shots, but he doesn't partake. He is polite to everyone, and I follow slowly behind him.

I break away when I spot Adrian, Bethany, Salem, and Savannah on the tailgate of Troy's truck. Adrian hands me a water bottle from her cooler after I hop onto the tailgate beside her.

"He looks like a politician," Salem states, nodding towards Hamilton in the crowd two trucks away.

"Yeah," I agree. "Everyone wants a moment with him before he leaves." A heavy weight settles in my chest. I'm not in the mood for this large crowd. I'd prefer my last evening with Hamilton to be just the nine of us somewhere we could chat and hear each other easily. "Where are the guys?" Savannah points them out on the other side of the bonfire.

A round of cheers erupts as country music begins to blare through large speakers in the bed of nearby truck, making it harder to hear each other. Hamilton finally arrives our tailgate. Adrian attempts to pass him a beer—he grabs a water bottle instead. I don't draw attention to it but wonder why he isn't drinking tonight. He always enjoys a couple of beers at parties.

Troy, Winston, and Latham return to our group. Ever the hostess, Adrian passes out cups of beer from the keg. Bethany pulls Troy between her legs and tugs his lips toward hers. Salem points to her lips, and Latham obediently kisses her, too.

"I'm going for a walk," I inform the group. "Hamilton, will you join me?"

We slip between the trucks to avoid the large crowd around the fire. As we walk away, the light of the fire grows faint, and the music fades. In the moonlight, we easily stroll near the water's edge.

"I'm going to miss this," Hamilton confesses, tossing sticks into the river.

Far enough we can no longer see the fire, I take a seat on a large log. I remove my flip-flops and dig my toes into the cool sand. Hamilton sits beside me. I need to confess the true reason I suggested a walk.

"I want you to promise me something," Hamilton states, eyes locked on mine. "I want you to put down the books and go out in Columbia. I want you to remember to have fun and enjoy the college experience. I'll never forgive myself if my being drafted ruins college for you." He places his hands on my shoulders, his arms fully extended, eyes still peering deep into mine. "Promise me you will make friends, go to games, leave the dorm and live. Yeah?"

I nod, knowing his fear is warranted. I planned to hang with him, and now he won't be attending MU. I've already vowed to take heavy class loads, buckle down, and graduate as fast as possible.

"Mady." He tugs my chin back up so our eyes meet. "I need you to promise me. I need to hear your voice."

He knows me too well. If I speak the words, I will keep my promise. "I promise I will attempt to make friends and attend a game or two." Even now, fear fills my stomach at the thought of putting myself out there with strangers. My words appease him; he smiles at me.

Now it's my turn to ask something of Hamilton. I don't want a promise—I want a favor. "I planned to ask a favor of you in August but need to ask you tonight instead." I wring my hands in my lap, struggling, to find the words. I thought I would have another two months before I needed to know the perfect words to urge him to assist me. I decide to just go for it. "Um, I want you to be my first." I witness the shock on his face. I'm a little relieved I don't see disgust and revulsion. This will be a true test of our friendship.

Hamilton leaps from the log. His eyes look anywhere but at me as he kicks at sand with the toe of his boot.

"I don't want some stupid college guy at a frat party to be the one." This is awkward. I growl in frustration. "You wouldn't want that for me, would you?"

I pause for a moment hoping for his agreement. He runs his hands through his hair then replaces his hat. He looks toward me as his lips part, then he quickly looks away. It's clear he's struggling for a reply.

"I want it to mean something. I don't want to be ashamed of it. I need it to be you."

Hamilton rubs his hands over his face, before pacing from one end of the log to the other. He clasps his hands together behind his neck, growling he looks up to the stars.

"How can you ask this of me? Seriously? Darn it, I mean, Madison, you are my best friend. If I granted your request," His eyes lock on mine. "We wouldn't be best friends anymore. I can't lose you." His hands on my jaws, his bold, brown eyes bore into mine. "I WON'T lose you. Although our plans have changed, I will still need you. We'll just use our phones more. Please don't ask this of me. I can't refuse you—I don't want to lose you."

"Just hear me out," I plead. "I'm not asking you to fall in love with me, I am just asking you to share a very important moment with me. It will mean more with you than some random guy I haven't met yet. I just can't go to college a virgin. I will be far from all of my friends, far from you. I won't have someone close to talk to. I didn't plan to be a virgin at eighteen. Heck, I haven't gone past over the shirt second base. I can't go to college like this. I worry that I might never..."

"You'll make new friends. You'll meet nice guys, guys worthy of you." Hamilton kneels in front of me, taking my hands in his. "You'll want to share this with one of them. It won't be some random guy at a frat party. I know you; frat parties won't be a common event for you."

"Please," I beg. "I want it to be you." I place my hand upon his cheek. His stubble prickles my palm. "Do this for me, please."

"It's time to go." Hamilton roughly pulls me up from the log and escorts me back toward the bonfire.

We say our goodbyes. Adrian raises a brow my way. I shake my head and she mouths "okay". Silently, following him, I return to Hamilton's truck. Without a word, we head down a dirt road, then a gravel road, before the blacktop, and then the highway. The silence allows my mind to worry. *Did we leave because he plans to honor my wish? Did we leave because he is tired and has a long drive tomorrow? Or did we leave because he is angry with me?*

"Madison…"

"Hamilton…" We speak at the same time causing us to chuckle.

He changes the radio from the local country station to a rock station for me. Mötley Crüe fills the cab. I refrain from speaking as he returns me to my car in the grocery lot.

I timidly wave goodbye as he pulls away. It's not like him to leave prior to ensuring my old car starts for me. As my car sputters to life, I kick myself for not speaking up during the drive. *I need to know if he's mad at me. I need to know I didn't just ruin the best thing in my life. I need to know if I just lost my best friend for asking a favor of him.* I pound my palms against my steering wheel in frustration.

NINETEEN

If you attempt to purchase condoms, you went to school with the checker, are related to the checker, or they are friends of your parents. It's just one of the 4,724 reasons I want to leave Athens.

MY THOUGHTS CONSUMING all of my attention, I don't remember the drive home. I really need to be more careful. As I pull myself from my car, I barely notice my mother's car is not in the driveway. Instead of cursing her as I begin to worry, I trudge up the sidewalk, in the unlocked front door, and down to my room. Huffing, I dramatically throw myself onto my bed. I stare at my ceiling for a couple of minutes.

I can't be here. It feels like the walls close in and the ceiling drops to crush me. I snag a bottle of water from the refrigerator, a quilt from the back of the sofa, and escape the house with all of its formerly happy memories now erased by my mother's addiction. As my feet follow the path I've taken hundreds of times, I allow myself to breath in the humid night air. Although it cooled twenty degrees from today's high, it's still nearly 80 degrees. I love summer nights. The bullfrogs croak loudly in the nearby pond. Crickets sing from the grass below my feet. Lightning bugs twinkle like the millions of stars in the midnight blue sky. On the way to my favorite spot, my mood lightens fractionally.

I scale the chain-link fence to enjoy my safe-haven. I spread my quilt near the base of the large oak tree in the center of the cemetery. I lay on my blanket, my eyes taking in the stars visible just outside the canopy of my tree, desperately wishing I wasn't alone in this moment. Only one person knows of my special spot and considering the excruciatingly quiet ride from the river to my car, I doubt he'll venture here tonight.

I believe everything happens for a reason. I feel if something is meant to be, opportunities will continue to present themselves until it occurs. People enter and exit our lives not by chance but by fate. It was fate that caused me to bump into Hamilton in the hallway in middle school. Fate threw us into several classes together. Then, fate sealed our friendship by revealing we share the same special spot at the cemetery where we found we lived on farms on opposite sides of it.

I try to convince myself that I am glad Hamilton will not be sharing this space with me tonight. I realize I need time to figure out how to undo the damage that I caused by asking a favor of my best friend. I only have eleven hours to undo the mess I made. Lying alone under my tree, surrounded by the headstones, is all I need while I search for remedies. I text Adrian. When she doesn't reply, I assume she's still at the party. I resign myself to the fact that I am alone in finding my solution to my request of Hamilton.

Saying goodbye to him tomorrow scares me in ways I never thought it would. He was to be my nearest and dearest until we were real adults with real jobs out in the real world. He entered my life for a reason. I would not have survived losing my dad and my mother's subsequent downward spiral without him by my side. I've leaned on him so much that the thought of my upcoming life changes without him causes panic.

Focus. How can I fix this? How can I fix us? I can't claim I consumed alcohol, and it was the alcohol talking. I can't play it off as a joke gone wrong since I didn't try to laugh it off in his presence. I could claim it was a dare, Adrian dared me to approach him on his last night in Athens. I'm not convinced he'd buy that. Think. Think. Think!

I sit up to sip from my water bottle, tilting my head to the side. I hear it, my favorite sound in the world, the only thing missing from this beautiful summer's night graces my ears. *Whip-poor-will, Whip-poor-will.* Usually only heard at dusk, I am thrilled this bird chose the middle of the night to sing. *Whip-poor-will, Whip-poor-will.* It's music to my ears. I lay back on my elbows, enjoying the entire setting. The warmth, the humidity, the sounds, the smells, the location, I allow it all to caress my soul.

Crack. Snap. I dart up at the sounds of something approaching. I turn my head, trying to decipher the direction of its approach. I'm somewhat safe within the chain-link fence. Fear prickles the hair on the back of my neck as I realize it is not an animal approaching.

Crap! It's Hamilton. As much as I want to undo the mess I created, I hoped I had a bit more time to come up with a strategy. As he approaches the fence to enter our safe place, I scramble to find words to greet him.

"Hey," he greets, placing his blanket next to mine.

"Hey."

Several long, quiet moments pass as we lie staring at the night sky.

"I'm gonna miss this." Hamilton's words are a punch to my gut. I pull my eyes from the heavens as I hear the rustling of Hamilton turning on his side to face me. "I'm gonna miss you."

"In a year, you'll be wearing a suit, riding in a car service, jetting all over the states and around the world." I turn on my side to face him. "You'll be so citified, you'll laugh at your redneck youth, your redneck friends, and the country life you once led. You'll enjoy blonde arm-candy everywhere you go. You'll be well on your way to a million-dollar house with a million-dollar family." *And you'll forget all about me*, I think to myself. My words leave an acrid taste in my mouth.

Hamilton's laughter pierces the night. I love his laugh. It's a full belly laugh. I'm gonna miss it.

"I may live in the big city. I may travel by jet, but I will never be citified." In the moonlight, I see traces of his smile. "I will always drive a truck. I will never enjoy arm-candy; if I make millions, I will invest for my future rather than spend it quickly, and I will never go a week without speaking to you." He presses the tip of my nose with his index finger.

I want to believe him, but I know friends drift apart after high school. Long distances between us will probably cause us to lose touch. His busy ball season and my course load will tug us in different directions.

"When my father died, and things were tough on the farm," his words and eyes hold me captive, "you refused to let me quit baseball to help Mom with the work. You're my number one fan." He chuckles. "You're the one that pushed me to put my name into the draft. I am who I am because of you. No matter what changes come in the upcoming year, I will not let you slip away."

I want to believe him. I want to keep him in my life forever. I need his friendship even at a distance.

"Come here," he prompts, pulling me tight to his chest.

With my face pressed to him, my nostrils fill with his masculine scent. Taking a deep inhale, I save it to memory.

"Did you just sniff me?" He laughs.

"Maybe."

I feel his laughter vibrate through his chest. I extricate myself from his hug, placing several inches between us. I need to see his face. I want to see his dark brown eyes.

Hamilton sighs. "I was serious about the promise you made me tonight."

Oh crap! Are we going to discuss his promise and my favor now? Crap! "I promised. I will make an effort and even send you proof."

"I don't need proof," he states. "You promised; that's all I need. I might remind you every now and then, but proof isn't necessary. Your word is all I need." He places his right hand on my forearm. "I need to ask something else from you. Tomorrow, at my house, with my mom, I need you to promise not to cry."

Judging by his reaction, I know my eyes bug out.

"My mom is really struggling with my leaving so soon. She's going to be a mess. I need you to be the strong one. I need you to help me. I'm going to attempt to make a quick exit. I think the longer I draw it out, the harder it will be for her."

I nod as words are caught behind the tears burning the back of my eyes and throat. I can do this for him. I can keep it together until the dust from his truck billows on the lane. I cannot promise to hold them off after that. I roll to my back, needing our surroundings to calm me. Hamilton mimics my movements.

"Hear my whippoorwill?" I ask, moving on to lighter topics. "You won't hear those in Des Moines or Chicago."

"I hear your annoying little friend," he teases. "He's probably warning you it's too late to be out and to go home."

"I can't go home." I confess what he already knows to be true.

"Not any better, huh?"

"She's staying out later and later," I admit. "She's out much later than the bars stay open. I don't want to even think of what that means."

"It's harsh, but you can't help her if she refuses the help." Hamilton's words ring true but do nothing to dissuade my guilt. "I can't help but think your life will start when you leave that house. You'll be free of her tirades and binges, no longer spending every minute at home worrying for her safety."

"True," I agree. "I worry that without me around, she'll hurt herself or others while under the influence. I'd like to think knowing I'm at home, a tiny part of her brain worries about me. With me gone, she will have nothing to guilt her into sober moments."

I don't know how long he's been doing it, but I notice Hamilton's fingers playing with my loose tendrils. We've shared emotional discussions in the past. This touch, his actions, seem much more intimate.

Turning my head towards him and into his hand, I look up through my lashes to find him gazing at me. He doesn't withdraw his hand. Instead, it cups my jaw while his thumb caresses my cheek.

"Are you nervous?" I ask, trying to make the moment less awkward.

"I'm excited, not so much nervous," Hamilton admits. "They've scouted me for more than a year. They have faith in me, so I just need to keep doing what I'm doing and see where it leads." He shrugs his shoulders.

His thumb pauses at the corner of my mouth. All the air evaporates around us. I can't breathe. I can't think. This touch is more intimate. My eyes are locked on his and my mind is focused on his thumb on my lips. I can't blink. I can't move. I should react, but I have no idea what to do.

"Breathe Madison," his deep voice murmurs.

I gulp in air like a fish out of water, still frozen in place. He gently brushes the pad of his thumb over my lower lip from one corner to the other. A gasp escapes. It's the clue he waited for. His lips collide with mine. In his kiss, I feel his need, his hunger. His plump lower lip is heavy and hot on mine.

When he pulls away, I'm left needing more, wanting more, desiring more. My eyes lock on his. His pupils dilate while watching my tongue slowly moisten my lip from one side to the other. Breath catches in my throat. His eyes on mine, he slowly brings his mouth to mine, pausing at the last moment to ensure my consent. I lean towards him.

His firm lips press to mine. His familiar scent surrounds me. It's unlike anything I've ever imagined.

As Hamilton's hand on the back of my neck secures my mouth to his, my hands abandon his hair, feather down his neck, and begin their descent over his hard chest. I fist my hands in his T-shirt at his abdomen. My need to hold on to him is fierce.

"PLEASE DON'T CRY." Hamilton's words make me aware of the warm streams of tears on each cheek. I frantically wipe them.

"I'm not sure why I'm crying," I chuckle in an attempt to make light of the tears. "I haven't cried since..."

"Since your dad's funeral." Hamilton finishes my sentence before wiping away a stray tear. He kisses the tip of my nose.

"I think they are happy tears."

Hamilton searches my face to access my honesty. "Did I hurt you?"

I shake my head.

"You never cease to amaze me with your words and actions. You'd think after five years I would be ready for it all." His words are music to my ears. He likes my honesty, my descriptions, and the way I live life. Warmth swells within me. I snuggle closer to Hamilton's chest with my back as he holds me in his arms. *Do I feel different as a woman? Not really.* It is silly of me to think I'd feel changed by losing my V-card. I won't dress or walk differently tomorrow. It's similar to my eighteenth birthday. Suddenly I was legally an adult but didn't feel any different. I still went to high school each day and worried about college in the fall, just as I won't change after tonight.

I'm so close to sleep. Lying wrapped in Hamilton's arms, snug to his chest, listening and feeling his steady breaths, this is bliss. Just as I begin to drift off, Hamilton's whisper tugs me back.

"It was better than I fantasized." Hamilton's sleepy masculine voice murmurs.

Wait what? He dreamt of this? Of me? When? "Better than I fantasized". Did my best friend Hamilton fantasize about being with me? Did he think about this before I asked a favor of him tonight? Crap! How do we go back to a friendship now? I feel things for Hamilton. They are the type of feelings best friends don't have. I crave him in a primal way. Hamilton tightens his arms around me as he shifts positions. I try to lie still. I'm a bit uncomfortable with my confused thoughts.

Hamilton's breathing is even as his limbs are heavy around me. After a few moments, I realize he's asleep. *Asleep? Was he talking in his sleep?* His confession about his fantasies for me remain an even bigger mystery.

"I'M SORRY," Hamilton whispers, stirring from sleep prior to kissing my shoulder. "I turn in his arms. He smiles, pulling me to his chest. "I'm sorry I messed up our plans." Hamilton states. "But really it is your fault. You pushed me to enter the draft this year instead of three to four years from now when I planned to. I honestly didn't believe I would be drafted. I hoped but never dreamed."

Hamilton always underestimates his true worth. He knows he is talented. He knows he can play college baseball. His dream of playing Major League Baseball is one he only shared with his parents and me. I encouraged him to enter the draft. It is my fault he will leave me tomorrow. His gift needs to be shared—I pushed him to enter, knowing others would recognize it, too.

Hamilton's fingers trace my smug smile. "You're proud of yourself, aren't you?" His thumb caresses my cheekbone. "You were relentless about the draft. I gave in just to shut you up. And now, I'm playing minor league baseball for the Chicago Cubs." He rolls to his back.

I place my hand upon his arm. "God blessed you with a rare gift in your left arm. He gave you the strength and love for the game to endure your greatness." I feel his muscles tighten as he makes a fist. "You've entertained Athens long enough. Soon you will entertain baseball fans everywhere."

Hamilton rolls to face me. He pulls me to his chest in a tight embrace. "You've always been my biggest fan."

"I still will be. I plan to follow you online, drive to Des Moines for a game or two, and I will even call to ride your butt if you slack off."

Hamilton places a chaste kiss on my forehead. Then his lips linger but a hair's breadth away from mine. I lift my eyes to meet his while my tongue peeks out to wet my lower lip. I blink. He lowers his head, and squeezes me tightly while releasing a deep sigh.

"As much as I hate for this to end, it is late, and we should head home." Hamilton continues to hug me.

We use our cell phone lights to gather our clothes. Once dressed, I hand Hamilton his hat.

"Uh, thanks." Hamilton's voice hesitates.

"Um, yeah." Words clog my throat while I dart my eyes over our surroundings. *This is the awkwardness I expected.* I stand hands on my hips not sure how to stand or what to say. I'm not sure what my body language expresses to him at this moment. *I am so out of my element here.*

Fortunately, Hamilton ends my discomfort. He says goodnight, I nod, and we walk in opposite directions. Tears fill my eyes as I realize this is probably the last time Hamilton and I will share our favorite place. Tomorrow, our lives venture down opposite forks in the road.

TWENTY

The newspaper comes out once a week—it's one of the 4,724 reasons I want to leave Athens.

"NO TEARS." Hamilton's words from last night play on a loop in my head. I need to focus on the positives, while I show my support and excitement for the ball games in his future. I exit my car, parked beside his large red truck in his driveway. Making my way onto the deck, I enter through the screen door, and into his home for the last time. I paint a smile upon my face.

"Good morning, Madison," Memphis greets. "Can I get you something to drink?" She looks tired. I doubt she slept last night. The redness ringing her eyes leads me to believe she's cried already today.

"I'll get it." I pull a cup from the cabinet and pour a glass of unsweetened iced tea. I scan the nearby family room for evidence of Hamilton. "Is he ready?" I hope she understands the many meanings of this question.

"He's all packed, and the truck is loaded." She scoots closer to my side, leans in, and whispers, "He's excited. We need to put on a brave face for his sake." She motions her head toward the stairs. "Why don't you run up and light a fire under his butt."

I nod, place my iced tea on the table, then climb the stairs to Hamilton's room as I have a million times before, reminding myself to smile with every step.

"You better get a move on if you plan to blow this pop stand by noon," I tease with all the faux excitement I can.

With duffle bag in hand he scans his bedroom one more time before motioning me to exit as he follows. I descend the steps, feeling the heaviness of his stare on my back. Thoughts of last night creep into the forefront of my mind. Thoughts of his hands, his lips, his tongue, his breath, and his body. His nearness heightens my senses. Although I promised nothing would change, I fear it has for me. I wonder if it has for him, too.

"There you are," his mother calls upon our reaching the kitchen. Her proud smile lights up her entire face.

Hamilton passes me to wrap his mother in a tight hug. He murmurs words, near her ear, I cannot make out. When he pulls away, she nods in agreement. Hamilton encourages the two of us to lead the way to his truck. I hope the smile I fake doesn't allow my fear and sadness to show. It feels as though I am walking the green mile to my death. Concrete hardens in my stomach. I want to change colleges and follow him to Des Moines. Hamilton happiness is the only thing keeping me from begging him not to leave me alone. I don't want to return to life without Hamilton by my side. *How will I ever adjust to college this fall without him? A big part of my life will end with his pickup truck driving away from us.*

I tuck my thumbs in the front pockets of my shorts. My eyes stare at my red Converse and the gravel around them. The toes of Hamilton's worn work boots enter my line of sight. I feel his stare. I sense his reluctance.

"Remember our promise?" he whispers.

"No tears," I murmur while raising my eyes to meet his. I don't feel like crying at this moment. I feel an open chasm in my chest. I struggle to breathe as the empty hole hurts more with each passing second.

Hamilton shakes his head. "The other promise," he prompts.

I'm unable to prevent the squinting of my eyes. The promise that I will struggle to keep. The promise to overcome my greatest fears, to make myself available to new friendships and activities. I purse my lips and nod.

Hamilton's long arms pull me tight to his chest. Turning my head to the side, I lay it upon his chest. I inhale his masculine scent. Tipping his head down, he whispers in my ear, "I'm still here for you. I'm only one text or call away. I hope you will be the same for me. I'm going to need my biggest fan now more than ever."

"I'm here for you." My voice is barely a whisper.

I smile as he breaks our embrace. I see the sparkle in his eyes as his smile lights his entire face. He cannot mask his excitement to play minor league baseball. I am excited for him, too.

As he opens his truck door and climbs in the cab, the aching hole in my chest burns. I jump when the truck door slams. The engine roars to life as Hamilton lowers his window. Memphis stands beside me, her arm over my shoulders. He waves goodbye before backing out of the driveway and disappearing down the lane.

Memphis' arm tightens, pulling me closer. "We'll get through this." Her words sound resolute. "I'll be here for you anytime, and I'm gonna need you to keep me company from time to time." She turns to face me. "I hope we can continue our Sunday trips to church and dinner together."

I nod, afraid of the sobs that might escape if I open my mouth. My heart feels made of stone; surrounding it is only emptiness, a large void. I ache.

TWENTY-ONE

The driver's license exam is only given one day a week. It's another of the 4,724 reasons I want to escape this town.

HAMILTON'S MOTHER leads me back into the kitchen, encouraging me to sit and enjoy my tea. She fixes a glass and joins me at the table. My eyes squint as they follow the slow movement of her hand pushing a blue envelope toward me.

"What's this?"

"All I know is Hamilton asked me to pass this to you after he left today." Her warm smile and brown eyes remind me of her son. I fear everything will remind me of him in the months to come.

I cannot contain my excitement as I open the flap and pull a card from the envelope. Bright flowers shine on the front as I read, "Roses are red. Violets are blue." I open the card, anxiously awaiting Hamilton's parting words of wisdom for me. Inside, I find a black sharpie has crossed out the printed words, and I spot his handwriting underneath. "I have planned a scavenger hunt for you." My brow furrows as I attempt to understand the words I read.

"Well?" his mother prompts. "What does it say?"

"I guess he planned a scavenger hunt for me."

As she laughs out loud, she points to a royal blue gift bag on top of the refrigerator. My name graces the gift tag in large black letters. I hop from my chair and bring the bag back to the table. I look to Memphis questioningly before I peek in the top of the bag. I pull out the notecard. I smile at Hamilton's messy print decorating both sides.

"Read it out loud," Memphis demands.

"I've prepared a series of clues to remind you how we came to be. A blue gift bag waits for you in every location. Clue #1: One day in September a nerd and a jock collided, I remember."

In my mind, I recreate the day we officially bumped into each other over and over which led to us talking which led to our friendship. In the busy middle school hallway, we collided on the way to our third period classes. My armful of books toppled to the floor and he scrambled to help me pick them all up. I thanked him, and we went our separate ways—or so we thought. Moments later he took the empty seat next to mine in math class. We found ourselves in three more classes together.

"The answer to the first clue is the middle school," I inform Memphis. "Would you like to come with me?"

"This is his gift to you," she states, shaking her head. "I'll want all the details when you are done."

I spring up from my seat, pat her on the shoulder, and hurry to my car. I am both nervous and excited to see what memories Hamilton found important enough to use as clues to entertain me this afternoon.

MY EYES SCAN the middle school parking lot as I exit the car. I'm looking for a blue bag. I'm not sure how big or small it might be.

There are so many places around the school he might have hidden the next clue that I worry I might not find it. As I slowly walk and scan the area, I contemplate inviting Adrian to assist me on the scavenger hunt. I decide to try it on my own first and call for help if I need it later.

I pass the main entrance then one side of the building before I stop to think. Hamilton and I found a squirrel's nest outside the language arts windows. We often watched the baby squirrels in the nest instead of reading as instructed in class. I jog to the opposite side of the building. At the base of the squirrel tree, I find the royal blue gift bag with my name on the tag.

Inside is a five-by-seven-inch wooden frame with pictures of Hamilton in his little league uniform and me in my softball uniform from the summer after eighth grade. I giggle at how goofy we were. Hamilton's smile reveals the space between his front teeth that braces later fixed. My thumb nail between my teeth as I smile, reminds me of the large zit I sported that day, that my hand covers.

The distressed, white-washed frame perfectly surrounds this photo. I pull out the notecard with my next clue.

"Clue #2: I begged my mother to take me to your softball game to cheer for you—the next week you returned the favor. Go to the place that sold more than one bubble gum flavor."

I return to my car with my gift in tow to drive to the concession stand near the city league ball fields. I loved sour apple gum. Hamilton preferred grape or original flavor. In the concession stand, they carried all three flavors. The nights his parents worked the concession stand, we conducted a test to see which flavor was more popular. I guessed it would be grape while Hamilton thought it was original. We counted every piece prior to opening the windows and then again after closing the stand. While the two of us watched ball games, his parents pulled half the tub of sour apple gum and hid it. When we finished counting, we were shocked that neither one of us was correct. His parents waited over a year before confessing they rigged our experiment.

On the ledge by the closed concession window, I spy the royal blue gift bag. Inside, I find a framed picture of the two of us. These photos are only a year old now, and I can see so many differences in the two of us. I clutch the frame to my chest as I pull out the next clue.

"Clue #3: On the day I passed my driver's test, I took you to the place with the drink you liked best."

The day Hamilton got his license, he drove me to Sonic Drive-In after school. I lived for their vanilla cola. He treated me to a large one before he drove me home.

I turn the card over. "Ask for today's special." This concerns me. They don't have daily specials. I don't ponder his rationale. I drive to Sonic, looking forward to ordering myself a vanilla cola to accompany today's special.

When I push the large red button to order, I nervously order "today's special". I hope the disembodied voice inside knows what my order means. Moments pass before a carhop delivers a large vanilla cola to my car. I attempt to pass my cash to her, but she informs me the drink has already been paid for. Then, she hands me a royal blue gift bag. Inside, I find a $25 Sonic gift card and my next clue.

"Clue #4: We started each day the same if practice didn't interfere. With our diploma we earned our way out of here."

I exit my parking stall, pull from Sonic back onto the main drag, and point my car to Athens High School. Although the district didn't assign parking spots, our group parked in the same slots every day and arrived early enough to hang out prior to the first bell.

I quickly see the royal blue gift bag in my parking spot for the last three years. Inside, I find a framed photo of the two of us that graced the back cover of our yearbook. Hamilton and I sit on his tailgate. I face Hamilton, a smile on my profile, as he faces the camera, laughing.

In this moment, captured by a yearbook staff member, I had just shared the story of slipping in the hog pen and ripping out my jeans doing chores that morning, early in our senior year. Our friend,

Savannah, claimed I should have showered again as I still smelled of the hog lot. Hamilton found this super funny.

I am not sure how long I lean on the hood of my car, staring at the two of us. My heart aches. I thought college would continue where high school left off, Hamilton and I sharing moments along the way in Columbia. The last 48 hours changed all of that. Our paths officially split today. I'm glad I now have these photos to remind me, but they are no replacement for him. I underestimated his importance in my life. *How will I ever make it on my own?*

"Clue #5: In eighth grade for each other we started to care. For we found we had more than classes to share."

My head tilts to the side as I reread this clue several times. We ran into each other in the hallway eighth grade year. We shared four classes together. We both liked sports. *What else did we SHARE?*

It's the cemetery Hamilton stumbled upon only the week before we met there. I accused him of stalking me. He found my accusation hilarious. We learned that we lived on opposite sides of the cemetery from each other. I used it to escape—he used it to dream. We kept our cemetery between the two of us.

Approaching the cemetery, under the large acorn tree I find the royal blue gift bag. My body tingles as I recall our actions last night. I shake off those thoughts as I focus on my scavenger hunt. I pull out a wrapped box and Hamilton's handwritten note. I read the words out loud.

"This is your final stop. Our shared favorite place sealed our friendship. Here I learned we were destined to be together." A sob escapes. We are no longer together. He follows his dream and I wonder what I should do now. "Although our journeys are hundreds of miles apart, as my best friend, you hold a special place in my heart. As you open my final gift, I know you'll be angry with me. I couldn't leave you today without a plan in place to ensure constant contact between the two of us. Now, open the gift and don't rant until you read the note inside."

Tears fall from my lashes to my cheeks and my hands tremble as I turn the rectangular box. It's heavy. I peel a corner of the paper away to reveal a white box. As I tear more, I find it's an iPhone box. *No way! He better not have.* I slide the lid from its base, unfold the paper, and read.

"We now share an unlimited plan. I expect you to use the hell out of the unlimited texts, calls, and data. Your number is the same. Transfer your contacts from your antiquated flip-phone before you toss it in the trash where it belonged years ago." I follow the arrow to flip the note over. "Cuss all you want, but you better call and text me from this gift tonight. Your BFF, Hamilton"

Damn him! As upset as I am that he spent so much money on me, I am beyond grateful. I can't afford to upgrade my plan or my cell phone, and my mother uses her money on liquids rather than me. I want to stay in our special place but scurry home to move my contacts into the new phone.

TWENTY-TWO

You run into your general practitioner, who is also your gynecologist, at church, at the store, and at restaurants. This is a very important reason I want to escape Athens.

AFTER SETTING up my new cell phone, I shoot a quick text to Hamilton.

Me: My what a busy boy you've been the last 48 hrs (smiling emoji)

I'M NOT sure of his schedule upon arriving in Des Moines. I imagine he would see the stadium, meet with the coach, and maybe practice with the team. I busy myself placing my new photo frames around my bedroom.

Hours later, my new iPhone plays *Centerfield* by John Fogerty, alerting me to Hamilton's text.

Hamilton: The emoji = new phone (smiling emoji)
Me: I (heart emoji) my gifts! Can't believe you had time
Hamilton: Adrian did photos & frames
Hamilton: Savannah bags & wrapped
Hamilton: Rest I did on my own
Me: You're going to make some girl (smiling emoji) some day

I CRINGE. *Why did I send that? It's bad enough he's a state away. If he gets a serious girlfriend...*My vibrating phone rescues me from that train of thought.

Hamilton: No time for chicks
Hamilton: they mess with my game
Me: Good boy
Hamilton: Boy? (Sad emoji)
Me: Good man
Hamilton: That's more like it
Hamilton: Time for practice
Hamilton: text or call you after
Me: sounds good

A FEW DAYS LATER, I select Nelson Sheridan from my contacts and dial.

"Mr. Sheridan's office, how may I help you?" a receptionist greets.

"May I speak with Nelson Sheridan please?"

"May I ask who is calling?"

"Tell him Hamilton Armstrong's number one fan is calling." She hedges a moment before placing me on hold. Maybe I should email instead of call. He might not take my phone call—I'm sure he is a busy guy.

"Madison, what can I do for you?" Nelson answers.

"I would like to help Hamilton's mother attend tomorrow night's game to see him pitch for the first time. I can drive her to Des Moines and back but need help securing tickets."

"I'll have my assistant secure two tickets for tomorrow night's game and leave them for you at the Will Call window in your name." I'm amazed how easy this was. I assume it's because Hamilton's an elite pitcher—with his talent comes the perks.

I quickly thank him. I cross tickets off my to do list. Up next is hotel room. I open Safari and search for hotels near the ballfield. *Where would I be without this new phone Hamilton gave me? Lost, that's where.* I reserve a room with two double beds. I cross hotel room off the list. All I need to do now is tell Memphis and pack.

I take a chance and drive over to the Armstrong farm. Memphis is watering her flower beds as I emerge from my car.

"Madison." She stands to greet me. "This is a surprise."

"No, the surprise is I have secured us two tickets to tomorrow night's I-Cubs game to watch Hamilton make his debut."

"Oh, Madison." I see the tears fill her eyes as her hand covers her mouth. "How? Where?"

"Let's sit on the porch swing." I prompt. As a gentle motion rocks us, Memphis is all ears. "I've arranged a room for us half a mile from the stadium. Nelson was happy to arrange tickets for us to pick up at will call."

The shock of my surprise wears off, and Memphis begins to plan.

"Let's take my car. Can we leave early enough to arrive during pre-game warm-ups?"

"Sounds good." I agree. "Let's keep it a surprise for Hamilton."

I STROLL up to the will call window, more nervous to watch this game than any before. I state my name and the staff member pulls an envelope from a nearby tub. But, before returning to the window, she makes a phone call. I can't hear her conversation from where I stand outside. I start to worry there might be an issue with our tickets. I fear we drove over three hours and now will not even see the game.

"Miss Crocker," a male voice calls from behind me. I turn. An older gentleman wearing a gold "Event Staff" shirt waits. I nod. "I'll escort you to your seats," he states before taking the envelope from the staff behind the window. "Please follow me."

Memphis and I grin at each other before following behind the large man. He walks us into the stadium then down closer to the field with every step. When I asked for tickets, I didn't plan on seats this close to the field. He pauses at the end of the first row of seats, at the far end of the home-team dugout. He hands me the two tickets and motions us to sit.

"The I-Cubs will be in this dugout. Pitchers warm up over here on this mound." He points to our left. The bullpen is just over the wall from the first row of seats. From our seats, we will have a perfect view of Hamilton warming up. "This is my section. I will be nearby. Please let me know if you need anything."

Memphis and I thank him for his help. When he walks away, we giggle and discuss how perfect our seats are. I am even more glad that we planned to arrive early to watch warm-ups. We head to the restroom then purchase beverages and snacks before returning to our seats.

When Memphis purchases a Snickers bar to keep Hamilton's pre-game ritual alive, I confess that I have a plastic bag in my pocket with a couple sunflower seeds, a sucker, a Milk-Dud, and a Mike & Ike. Laughing, we decide we are true baseball fans.

The teams are on the field warming up. Some run, some throw, and others stretch. Our eyes focus on the door in the outfield wall each time it opens. We've seen several team members emerge from it and are eager to catch our first glimpse of Hamilton.

I nudge Memphis when I witness a catcher appear, wearing his gear, followed by two players. As we watch, they spread out more, and we have our first sight of Hamilton. He looks tall and strong in his new uniform. Blue is definitely his color. He smiles as he walks and talks to the other players. It warms my heart to see him happy.

On the foul line, the three stretch and sprint a few times before playing catch. With each throw, Hamilton moves farther and farther away from his catcher on the line. It seems the third man is not a player but a coach. Perhaps he's the pitching coach. He walks by us into the dugout for a moment then returns to the catcher.

When Hamilton jogs over to his catcher, we watch as the three talk. The coach turns and points towards the dugout. Hamilton and the catcher crane their necks, looking where the coach points. In the moment Hamilton's smile turns megawatt, I realize the coach was pointing at us, not the dugout. Hamilton pats the catcher on the back before jogging towards us.

"He's coming." Memphis excitedly grasps my arm.

"This is a surprise," Hamilton states as he reaches over the wall to hug Memphis when she bends down.

"Surprise," I fake cheer.

"Did I miss a voicemail or a text?" he asks.

"No," Memphis replies. "Is it okay we came? We don't want to make you nervous."

"Mom," Hamilton's deep voice soothes. "I love you at my games. I want you at my games. If I had my way, the two of you would attend every game." His words are perfect. They are everything Memphis and I hope for.

Memphis slides the Snickers bar from her purse and hands it to Hamilton. He chuckles as the catcher and coach walk up behind him.

"What's this?" the coach asks, pointing to the candy bar.

"Just a pre-game ritual," Hamilton replies.

"Armstrong, where are your manners?" the catcher teases. "Introduce us."

Hamilton shakes his head. "This is my mother Memphis, and this is my number one fan, Madison." He tugs on the hem of my new I-Cubs jersey.

The coach greets us. The catcher nudges Hamilton. "I thought you said you didn't have a girl back home."

I snort. Yes. Making a great impression, I snort at his words. "I'm Hamilton's best friend, Madison. And although he left many broken hearts in Athens, I am not among them." I hope my words sound believable.

I don't hear the catcher's next words but laugh when the coach swats him on the back of the head and quickly maneuvers between the two players. Hamilton looks ready to kill him. I assume he made a comment about dating me or hooking up. After a few calming words, the catcher apologizes and ducks into the dugout. The coach asks if there are any other pre-game rituals he needs to be aware of before excusing himself.

"I'm so glad the two of you are here." Hamilton's brown eyes twinkle. He loves this game, and he loves his momma. "I need to go warm up, but hang around after the game. I'd like to see you." When we agree, he heads over to the bullpen area.

Memphis and I watch with rapt attention every pitch that Hamilton throws. Having watched him pitch for years, I can make out his slider, his curve, and his fastball. He looks a little tight. His pitches are on target; it's his stance that seems off.

The pitching coach heads back to the dugout while Hamilton tosses a few more to his catcher. Stopping in front of us, he asks, "How's he look?"

This catches me off guard. *Is he just making small talk, or does he really want to know?* I decide I need to do what is best for Hamilton. "You really want to know?"

At his nod, I share, "Pitches look good, but he is tight." I now have the coach's full attention. "It's his upper back--in his stance." I pause before continuing. "He probably needs to stretch his back more."

"If anyone can spot a difference in his stance, it would be Madison." Memphis states.

It's why I'm known as his biggest fan. My chest warms with Memphis' praise. It's as if she's a proud mom, and I am her daughter.

Coach hollers into the dugout. A trainer appears at his side before jogging to Hamilton. I hesitantly wave when Hamilton looks my way. I hope I didn't over step. He is now in the minor leagues—he probably doesn't want a friend telling his coach what he needs. Hamilton smiles and shakes his head at me before following the trainer back into the locker room. He's inside about ten minutes. I fret and stew the entire time.

When they emerge, Hamilton takes the bullpen mound again to throw a few more pitches. I smirk as it's now fixed. Maybe it's me, but it seems there is more pop when the ball hits the catcher's mitt. The catcher slings his arm around Hamilton's back. The two laugh as they walk and talk.

"I need to get me a number one fan," the catcher states when the two stand before our seats. He waves to us, pats Hamilton on the back, and disappears into the dugout.

"I needed an adjustment," Hamilton confesses, a smirk upon his face. "Thank you for pointing it out. I thought it was just nerves. But it's all better now."

I can only smile. We wish him good luck before he joins his teammates in the dugout.

TWENTY-THREE

The only books sold in town are textbooks at the community college and book orders through the elementary school—it's one of the 4,724 reasons I need to leave Athens.

WE STAND as the teams are announced. When Hamilton's name is called, he hops from the dugout onto the field. The crowd roars a welcome for their new pitcher. He turns to wave at his new fans, a wide smile upon his face. He's the luckiest man alive—he gets paid to play the game he loves. He winks our way before turning his back and assuming his place near the mound.

Goosebumps cover my entire body during the National Anthem. I squeeze Memphis' hand—she pulls me into a side-hug. My nerves ratchet higher as He takes his warm-up pitches upon the mound. He looks like the same man that took the mound in Athens less than a week ago. I would be a blubbering mess in his shoes. The pressures of a new league and level of play would be too much for me. Add to that coaches that are also his boss, large stadiums, bigger crowds, and tougher opponents. How he looks as he always does on the mound, I have no idea.

The umpire signals to Hamilton to start the game. Hamilton scans his fielders before assuming his throne on the white rubber. He studies the signs his catcher signals between his legs. With a slight nod, Hamilton agrees with his catcher. I grin as my favorite player delivers his first minor league pitch across the plate. The umpire calls strike. I glance to the scoreboard. His first minor league pitch is a ninety-three mile per hour fastball for a strike, a perfect start to this part of his baseball career.

Memphis and I cheer along with the I-Cubs fans surrounding us. I notice a difference in this crowd compared to the games I've attended. It seems the entire crowd supports the home team. These are now Hamilton's fans in Hamilton's new city. I hope they treat him well.

In his first inning, Hamilton throws ten pitches for two strike-outs and a ground-out. His new fans cheer loudly. Many on our side of the field call to Hamilton by name with congratulations. Hamilton smiles towards the stands before ducking into the dugout.

In the bottom of the sixth, the coach pulls Hamilton after two-thirds of an inning. I mentally tally his stats while I watch him wave to the crowd and disappear below. He earned fourteen strike outs, gave up one hit, and walked one. The I-Cubs hold a two to nothing lead as a right-handed closer assumes the mound. I am so proud of Hamilton's strong performance. I see good things in his future.

MEMPHIS and I stand at the wall, cheering with the other I-Cubs fans for the two to one victory. Hamilton gets the win, adding more icing on the cake of his first outing for the Cubs franchise. Hamilton asks us to meet him at the players' entrance, and our Event Staff member returns to escort us to meet him. As we walk, he comments on Hamilton's pitching and stats. I hope all the fans are this impressed with Hamilton on their team.

Our guide remains with us for the twenty minutes it takes Hamilton to join us. He shakes Hamilton's hand and says goodbye to us. Teammates invite Hamilton to join them at a local bar to celebrate. I know it's important for him to bond with the team, but I want to spend some time with him, too.

Hamilton states he will join them in half an hour. He throws an arm over Memphis' and my shoulder. "Let's go somewhere we can visit, someplace quiet." When we agree, he asks us to follow him back to his condo nearby.

OUR TIME at Hamilton's condo passes quickly. He animatedly shares stories of practices then the locker room and dugout of tonight's game. It's easy to see he is exactly where he is meant to be. The butterflies fluttering in my abdomen during the game and in his presence morph heavily into the pit of my stomach as the end of our visit draws near. *Goodbye's don't get any easier, do they?* I want to instruct Memphis to leave me here. I long to remain in Des Moines sneaking time with Hamilton while he's away from the ball park. I ponder giving up my goal of teaching to find a job nearby and attend all of Hamilton's games. The idea of being his groupie suddenly appeals to me. All I need to be happy is to be in his presence. Nothing else matters.

TWENTY-FOUR

The biggest employer in Athens is the school district followed by the grocery store. This is one of the 4,724 reasons I want to escape this town.

I'M EXCITED for my friends today as they start summer classes at Athens Community College. I decide to send them a text.

Me: 1st day of college-Go For It!
Me: I wish I was starting class
Me: I'm jealous
Adrian: have a great 1st day at ACC
Bethany: Thanks
Troy: Stop bragging you don't have school
Salem: Thank you

HOURS LATER, as I drive to Adrian's store, my phone vibrates with a group text from Adrian.

Adrian: regret not going college?
Winston: No, we have businesses to run
Winston: No time for classes. You regret it?

I REALIZE Adrian didn't mean to include me in the text, so I refrain from responding. I feel like a spy reading their conversation.

Adrian: No! Hate school, you know that
Adrian: Just miss time with the gang
Winston: They're not in same classes
Winston: we're together nights & weekends
Adrian: Not the same without Hamilton
Adrian: Madison leaves soon
Winston: Change is hard
Winston: our friendships won't change
Adrian: I know…Just sentimental today
Winston: I'm on my way to you
Winston: Bringing lunch
Adrian: (heart emoji)

CRAP! I already purchased lunch for Adrian and me.

"I COME WITH LUNCH," I declare, walking towards the counter.

"I have lunch, too." Winston chuckles before claiming we'll have a buffet to choose from.

Adrian assists in arranging Winston's deli sandwiches, chips, and slice of pie with my pizza, plates, and utensils. I remind them cold pizza will make a good snack later or for breakfast tomorrow.

Adrian enjoys lunch with the two of us. I don't look forward to leaving her for college. I know I need to spend as much time with her now while I can.

I'm not sure how he does it, but Winston weasels himself closer and closer to Adrian every day. It seems Adrian enjoys and looks forward to his company. She depends on him and seeks his input.

TWENTY-FIVE

Adults contact each other to compare the amount of rain in their rain gauges. Another of the 4,724 reasons I want to leave this town.

WEEKS PASS. Hamilton and I text or call each other daily. I'm about a month away from move-in day at college. I can't sleep. Tired of tossing and turning, I climb the stairs from the basement hoping not to see my mother. Walking through the living room, I spot a stranger sleeping on the sofa. Two empty bottles lie on the floor. Seems my mother didn't return home alone. I lock the bathroom door for privacy while I relieve myself. It's not bad enough I hide from my mother in my own home, now I have another to avoid. I tiptoe to the kitchen for water before returning to the safety of my bedroom. I don't dare make any noise—I don't want to deal with two drunks tonight.

As I sip from my water glass at the sink, a naked man opens the refrigerator door. I freeze and quickly realize this is not the man from the sofa. I shield my eyes as I excuse myself. I nearly stumble twice as

I scramble down the stairs. Earlier tonight, I felt relieved when GPS showed she made it home safely. Now I stand panic-stricken in my own room behind a locked door. So many times, I've felt like a prisoner in this house. I'm a prisoner of her alcoholism. I spend my evenings and nights worrying over her, looking up her location, and praying she makes it home without any harm. She's spent many nights in town. I realize she's stayed with men, tonight she flaunted it right in front of me. She's brought even more danger and stress into my life.

I can no longer deny her recklessness with her drinking and the giving of her body to others. Rage boils inside my belly at her thoughtlessness. Her years of neglect and destructive behaviors have hardened my heart. I still need my mother but can no longer be a part of her toxic life. I throw items into a backpack. I throw it over my shoulder, snag my phone and charger, then dart to my car.

The winds are picking up and I see lightning approaching from the west as I back from my driveway. While I drive the two gravel roads between my home and Hamilton's, I make a plan. I will tape a note to Memphis' bedroom door and her refrigerator letting her know I am sleeping in Hamilton's room. If I text she might wake up and I don't want her to be afraid if she hears me upstairs. I'll need to share everything with her tomorrow. For tonight, I will be safe. I just hope I can fall asleep.

MY VIBRATING PHONE WAKES ME. "HELLO," I mumble, not even looking at the caller ID.

"Why are you sleeping in my bed?" Hamilton's deep voice greets.

"How..."

"My mother texted me when she found your notes this morning. Now, stop stalling and tell me what is wrong."

"I didn't feel safe, and your house was the only one I felt I could run to in the middle of the night. I knew the doors would be unlocked, and Memphis wouldn't mind my intrusion," I confess.

"Did they...?" Hamilton's voice breaks at the thought of what drunk men might have done to me.

"No, I made sure to go straight to my room and lock the door." It kills me that he might have such a horrible thought. "I'm a big girl; I can take care of myself."

"I know that," he quickly replies. "I just...it enrages me that your mother put you in such a dangerous position. They could have done anything while she was passed out in her bedroom."

"Hamilton, please stop thinking about that." I can't have him upset over something that didn't happen. He has games to worry about. "I'm going to talk with your mother in hopes that I might be able to stay here for a while."

"You can stay until you leave for college," Hamilton firmly states. "My mother and I have talked about your mother in the past. I know she will have no problem with you staying. In fact, she's a bit lonely in my absence and will enjoy your company."

"I should probably head downstairs to chat with her. I am sure she is very worried." I don't want to let him go, but know he has things to tend to on his end, too. "Good luck tonight."

I ATTEMPT to call my mother around 2:00 p.m. Of course, she refuses to answer. I use my GPS app to ensure she is still at home before I shoot her a text.

Me: I'll be staying at the Armstrong's for a while
Me: Your 2 guests scared me last night
Me: 1 was naked in kitchen with me
Me: I didn't feel safe, so escaped
Me: text or call me please

"EVERYTHING OKAY, DEAR?" Memphis queries from outside my car window.

"Just trying to contact Mom." I pop my trunk before exiting the car. "I have a few groceries. Do you mind helping me carry them in?"

Memphis is not happy I thought I needed to chip in on food while I stayed with her. As we put the groceries away, I ask if I might prepare supper for us before Hamilton's game this evening. I'm glad to have someone to understand my constant refreshing of my browser for updates during the I-Cubs game.

While I cook, Memphis answers her cell phone. "Good afternoon," she greets. I listen to her side of the conversation as I fix myself a bowl of cereal. "My rain gauge had an inch and three-quarters in it when I woke this morning." Another pause then she parrots the caller's words, "Only a half inch, really? Well, it is better than nothing at all." I busy myself looking out the kitchen window for the rest of the conversation.

I smile, knowing I'll move to college soon. A new life awaits me in Columbia. I want to live in a world where daily life doesn't revolve around the moisture in the ground for crops.

BEFORE I TURN in for the night, I text Hamilton.

Me: Great game tonight!
Me: Ate popcorn & followed score online with your mom
Me: We had fun
Hamilton: How are you doing?
Me: Tried to reach mom, no luck
Me: so left her a message

Me: plan to stay here indefinitely
Hamilton: If I was there I'd confront her
Me: That never works with her
Hamilton: Are you sure you're ok?
Me: Better than I was at home
Me: Very cozy here
Me: Enjoy your mom's company
Me: I made street tacos for us for dinner
Hamilton: Never made me dinner
Me: Never asked
Hamilton: you didn't give her food poisoning?
Me: Nice
Me: Group of us will be at game next time on the mound in Des Moines
Me: Will send details in next day or 2
Hamilton: can't wait to see everyone
Hamilton; Got to go I need to load the bus
Me: Safe travels, get some sleep

TWENTY-SIX

A stranger driving through or visiting town quickly becomes hot gossip. This is one of the 4,724 reasons I want to escape this town.

ADRIAN VIDEO CALLS me late the next afternoon.

"My nerves are kicking into high gear the closer to the time for Winston to arrive draws near. I'm not sure why I agreed to attend dinner with him tonight at his parents' house. I mean, I've enjoyed our time spent together getting my store ready. I enjoy that we share similar goals for the next year and beyond. While all my friends go to college classes, we chose to work full-time on our businesses. There's something about dining with his parents that seems more like a couple than just friends. He claims this is not a date, just a casual dinner to discuss business. What do you think?"

"What should I wear? I think my definition of casual and Winston's family's might be very different. Should I wear my simple yellow sundress that has pale green flowers with my ballet flats?"

"That's perfect." It's funny that I am giving fashion advice for a dinner with a guy. I've never dated, let alone attended a dinner with a guy's parents. She's usually the clothing advice queen for our group.

Adrian actually squeals, causing me to jump, as her doorbell rings, signaling Winston has arrived.

"Adrian," her mother calls from the front door.

"Take a breath, you've got this." I marvel as my always confident friend is nervous about a guy for the first time. "Just be the Adrian we all love and have fun."

She quickly ends the video call.

TWENTY-SEVEN

It is common for a tractor or combine to drive down main street in the middle of the day. Just another one of the 4,724 reasons I want to wave goodbye to Athens.

THE NEXT MORNING, as I piddle around my bedroom, a text alert pings my phone.

Adrian: Need to talk
Adrian: can you swing by the store today

NOT EVEN BOTHERING TO REPLY, I throw on some jeans and head into town. At her store I find Adrian is all out of sorts. Her appearance is disheveled, and her body language displays signs of stress. It could be the daily stress of running her store, but I fear it is something else. My friend is in need, and I'm going to get the bottom of this.

"Spill it," I demand, placing my hand on her shoulder.

"I may have done something very stupid." Adrian fiddles with a pile of paperclips on the counter in front of us. "I broke a rule, and you're going to be so mad at me."

The sound of the bell above the front door of the store interrupts her confession. "Delivery for Adrian Slater," a young man calls as he approaches with a dozen red roses and baby's breath in a large glass vase.

I take the roses and slip a tip in his hand. I bite my lip in an attempt to hide the rather large, knowing smile upon my face. I place the vase in front of Adrian on the counter, spinning it so the card is right in front of her. She pulls the card from the tiny envelope.

"You slept with Winston, didn't you?" I state more than ask.

She clutches the card to her chest as her eyes dart to me from the opposite side of the counter. The look on her face asks me how I know without her telling me.

"There are only three possibilities with which you might have broken a rule and made me mad at you." I signal air-quotes with the word mad. "Hamilton is in Des Moines, played a game last night, then according to the texts we shared until 2 a.m. was on a bus with his team headed to Tennessee for tonight's game." I hold up my fingers. "So that leaves two options. Although I would be very happy for you to have hooked-up with Savannah last night, neither of you swing that way, and she would *not* have sent you roses today." I hold up my index finger. "That leaves one possibility. The two of you have spent a lot of time together setting up your business. You've made it no secret in the past that you find him hot. Therefore, I know you hooked-up with Winston last night. And where do you go from here?"

"Crap, woman! Enough of the third degree!" Adrian places the card back in the roses before she signals me to sit with her behind the counter.

"We had dinner with his parents last night. It wasn't just the four of us. So, we snuck out; then we went to the park to walk and ended up on the swings."

I nod my head, encouraging her to continue.

"Winston pulled me in for a kiss, things got heated, we drove, we parked, and I attacked him." Adrian attempts to summarize the evening in a brief synopsis.

I know her too well. She's having second thoughts about last night. "Nice try," I chuckle. "Let's start over, and if I'm to help you, I'll need *most* of the details." My friend tends to overshare of her sexual encounters. I don't need to hear about my friend Winston.

Adrian's eyes fog over as she settles in to share the entire evening with me. "When we hung up from our call, I descended the stairs happy to find Winston in gray plaid golf shorts with a solid Heather gray shirt and matching Sperrys. I smiled, knowing my sundress was a wise choice for the evening. Winston met me at the bottom step, commenting on my beauty. I remind myself 'he claimed this was not a date'. My mother told us to have fun as we walked to Winston's truck. In the safety of the truck cab, my nerves grew knowing a short drive then we would be at his parents' place."

"I asked him what was for dinner to break the awkward silence. He stated he wasn't sure. His mother asked that he invite me to dinner, so the two of us could share all we've accomplished for the store."

When we turned onto Winston's street, I noticed several vehicles parked on both sides of the little road. Winston commented that someone must be having a barbecue in the neighborhood. In the driveway, he turned to face me after he turned off his truck. He placed his hand on my forearm, smiled my way, and urged me to just be myself. He reminded me I'd met his parents before, and they loved me. Then, he stated it's just a simple dinner with some talk about my new store." Adrian smiles at me. "He was very sweet."

"I figured there's no time like the present to start the awkward evening, so I opened my truck door. Winston jogged to meet me at the front of the truck and took my hand in his. I had no time to contemplate the meaning of such a gesture, as his mother popped her head out the front door." Adrian's eyebrows rise, while she looks for my reaction to Winston's hand holding. I prompt her to continue, as I need more details before I can assume Winston's motives.

"She acted excited we were there with a smile on her face as she invited us to follow her. Imagine my horror when a large group yelled, surprise. A simple, casual dinner with his parents-my ass. What the heck? At the time I was sure Winston knew all about this dinner party and knew I would never agree to accompany him if he told me."

"Winston's voice immediately caught my attention, as he approached his mom seeking an explanation. His mother merely pulled Winston further into the family room toward the guests, claiming It's just a little surprise party to celebrate him taking over the theater. He quickly turned to me, swearing he didn't know." Adrian sighs dramatically. "His expression matched his words and he apologized to me. I barely had time to believe him before the crowd engulfed him, and I was pushed away from his side. When I scanned the crowd, I noticed many people I knew but have never socialized with."

"Winston's father rescued me by handing me a bottle of chilled water as I took a seat beside him on the sofa. He explained his wife got carried away. He told her Winston would hate this but claimed there was no stopping her when she had an idea. He told her she should contact me, so I was in on the secret, but he could tell by my shock that she neglected to do it.

"He ushered me out back. Large banners and balloons hung on the wooden privacy fence. The tablecloths, balloons, napkins, and cups all matched. I took a seat in a comfortable lounge chair on the outside of the patio seating area. While the crowd funneled into the backyard, Winston smiled my way attempting to walk over. Of course, he was stopped by several adults to congratulate him for taking over the family business. I felt out of place. If I had driven my own car, I would have left."

"When his father announced it was time to eat at the large grill, Winston directed me to join him at a table with his mother. He filled a plate for me." She pauses, scanning my reaction. "Can you believe that? Who does that? No *friend* of mine would ever do that." I nod and Adrian continues.

"I noticed several guests filter out the side gate during the meal. Winston's mother commented on my dress and about all the details he had shared with her about my store. I invited her to stop by and take a peek. I asked Winston to bring his parents by sometime." She shrugs. "I felt like they thought I was his girlfriend. It was kind of awkward."

"After dinner the crowd thinned. Winston decided we'd been there long enough and pushed me towards the door. I stated we should say goodbye to his parents before we left, he didn't agree. He stated they were enjoying time with their friends and he'd see them later."

"When he pulled from the drive he headed the opposite direction from my house. He stated he was embarrassed and sorry his mother sprung this upon us. He even claimed he was really looking forward to it just being the four of us. My stomach began to flutter at his actions. He wasn't the same Winston we've hung around with during high school. I couldn't tell, at first, if I liked the change or not." Adrian absentmindedly fiddled with a stack of papers on the sales counter.

"When Winston turned off the truck, we were at the city park. He exited the truck, jogged to my side, opened my door, and helped me step down. Hand-in-hand again we walked through the grass and trees towards the playground."

"You know me, I like to control situations. I felt anything but in control last night. The more he touched me and the sweeter he became, I felt more and more awkward. So, I let go of his hand and took a seat on the swing. I motioned my head to the empty seat beside me for Winston to join me and pushed off the ground. I love swings. I pumped my legs back and forth climbing higher and higher. Slowly I felt my control returning. I tucked my dress tight around my thighs to prevent any unwanted wardrobe malfunctions. Winston kept his feet on the ground, barely moving forward and back. When our eyes met —he was smiling."

"I taunted him to join me as I swung past him." A smile slips onto Adrian's face at the memory. "His serious face prompted me to still my pumping legs and drag my toes to slow down. As I halted my swing and spun it sideways to face Winston, he extended his arms, grasped onto the metal chains of my swing, and pulled me towards him."

Adrian's voice lowers to near a whisper. "His intense stare caught me off guard. Before I could decipher it, his lips latched onto mine in a slow, simmering kiss. As the kiss heated, my body grew hotter and hotter." Her eyes search mine.

"So, you liked Winston kissing you?" I smile approvingly.

Now begins the portion of Adrian's story that I dread hearing. In order to help my friend, decipher her interactions with Winston last night, I need to know what happened. I hate hearing intimate details since Winston is my friend, it's awkward. How will I ever look him in the eye after Adrian reveals these details? There are some things I don't need to know about him. Leave it to Adrian to share every tiny detail while enjoying my embarrassment.

In her eyes I see a hint of vulnerability. *This is new. My brave, strong, empowered friend for the first time has met her match.* Silently I nod for her to continue her story.

"He attempted to control his breathing, then suggested we get out of there." She smiles, taking a breath. "Those are my favorite five words or at least they are now my favorite. I have no idea if anyone witnessed our little swing make-out session. At that moment I didn't care." Adrian giggles. "We scurried to the pickup truck needing the privacy its cab could provide. Winston opened the passenger door, placed his hands on my hips, and he lifted me up to the seat. I longed to melt in my seat as I watched him eagerly round the truck to the driver's door. Instead, I slid across the bench seat needing to close the distance between us as he drove." She shakes her head. "I vowed I would never be *that girl*. I can't stand when needy girls cling to their man as he drives his truck. My body betrayed me. I had no idea where we drove. As you know, we both live with our parents. I trusted he had a plan."

"I must confess I love, love, love the fire Winston has ignited within me. Why haven't I encouraged him before last night? Winston has always been a hottie. His commanding presence exudes sexuality. Until now, I've never found an alpha appealing. I tend to be the dominate one, I make the first move, and I control every aspect of my relationships." Adrian shrugs, pretending to be embarrassed. "I know Winston well enough to know he's always in control. I've enjoyed our work together on the business. What if I can't submit to him? What if he won't submit to me?"

I offer no answers or insight to my friend. I need to know the rest of the last night's events. "Adrian, I need more information about last night. I will try to help you when you finish."

I continue to listen but resist visualizing my two friends together. While I've heard Adrian share her sex-capades in the past, this time is different. I've had my own experience with Hamilton now. Her descriptions bring back memories, feelings, and my body reacts. I struggle to focus on her to help her. I mentally gather my willpower to listen instead of daydream of Hamilton. *Listen, don't visualize. Listen, don't visualize.* I chant to myself.

Adrian never ceases to amaze me how comfortable she is with her sexuality or her private life. I never share such private matters with her or any of my friends. My cheeks heat. I'm sure she enjoys my discomfort as she shares her porno-esque retelling.

Surely, she is almost done. There cannot be much more to their evening.

Adrian resumes, and I continue to listen but not retain any of the details.

"It was such a perfect warm, clear night sky." Her dreamy voice pauses.

I place my hand lightly on her shoulder. This draws Adrian's attention from her daydream.

"I pulled his arm tight around my belly. Voices of reason flooded back to me. I asked him where this left us. I'm not one to regret sexual encounters, I need Winston's friendship, he's part of our group of nine, and feared I might lose it all."

"His warm breath still warmed my neck. He struggled for words as he tried to whisper near my ear. He said I'm hot, and he thought I was hot for years. He claimed he even told me that I was hot. He needed me as a friend, and he couldn't lose me. I turned in his arms to face him. I reminded him he knew me, when I wanted something, I took it, and when I liked something, I admitted it. I confessed I liked him, and I *really* liked being with him."

Adrian shakes her head. "His grin was barely visible in the light of the night when he mentioned we could try to be friends with benefits. I pressed my index finger into his chest for emphasis. 'Friends with benefits.' Can you believe he wanted me to be friends with benefits? When I didn't answer his grin was gone. He asked what I had in mind."

"I tried to quickly decide what I wanted. I confessed I didn't know, I needed time to think. I cuddled a little closer to his chest. I admitted that I liked that I didn't scare him when I came on a bit strong. He informed me; I do scare the crap out of him. His laugh was contagious as we lay in each other's arms."

Adrian sighs heavily running a hand through her messy hair. "Madison, I have never, and I mean *never*, been kissed like that before. It was slow, it was smooth, it was hot, and it reached to every cell in my body."

I smirk. Before June, I would not have understood that such a kiss could exist. After Hamilton's kisses, I know exactly what she means. I tuck my memories of Hamilton away; I focus on her at this moment. "So, this magic kiss swept you off your feet."

My best friend enjoyed her share of hook-ups during high school. But not once did she describe an encounter with these oohey-goohey emotions tied to it. Last night meant something to her. "Please tell me you didn't get R-rated on the playground of the city park."

"We kept it PG-13 while at the park." She traces an X over her heart with her index finger. She sighs a dreamy sigh at the memory. Adrian rises from her chair to stare out the front window nearby.

"The poor guy didn't stand a chance," I tease. Adrian is the type of woman that just goes for what she wants. I'm a little worried for Winston's condition after last night. He doesn't strike me as they type of guy that likes to be topped.

"Honestly, I was so wrapped up in how I felt and what I wanted that I didn't consider his needs at all." She turns to face me, leaning her arms on the counter. We even spooned. You know, like old people. I didn't know it could feel so good. While he clutched me to his chest, we asked where we go from here, and we didn't have an answer." She shrugs as if it is no big deal.

"It might be hard on the two of you and all your joint friends if it was a one-night stand. Dating is good, I think. So, when is he taking you out?"

"He's not."

I'm confused. My brow furrows, and I tilt my head. "You're not going out with him?"

She explains she told him she needed time to think about it. He knows she likes control and is impulsive—he's letting her lead.

I challenge her. "What's with all the uncertainty?"

"I've never allowed myself to feel this much before. He woke something in me, and now my world is all kinds of mixed up." She swirls her hands around her head, in demonstration.

"Adrian, I think that's a good thing. I know this scares you, but it also makes you feel alive. You're over-thinking everything. It's like you're a junkie, and you constantly need a fix." My words of understanding describe my feelings towards Hamilton after our night together. Unfortunately, unlike Adrian's situation, I won't have the opportunity to see Hamilton every day. "You should go for it. Just enjoy the ride."

"How do you know so much about this?"

I understand her question. She knows I barely went on any dates in high school. She believes I'm a novice. "I've read my share of romance novels. I've even read a few erotic romance titles." None of it's really a lie. Just an omission of truth. I'm just not ready to tell her about Hamilton. "I'm not mad at you. I'm actually excited for you. If I knew Winston would be this good for you, I would have set the two of you up a year ago."

"So, you think I should date him?" When I nod, Adrian continues. "What if it doesn't work out? Right now, we might just have the awkwardness of a night together. If we date, it could come between Winston and me while it effects all nine of us."

"Stop being a wimp." I blurt. "Go on dates. Make public displays of affection. Adrian, you have to give it a shot. Feelings like last night don't happen every day. You know this. You've shared details in the past. You can't let the potential for happiness slide through your fingers."

"Okay, Mom. Geez." she expresses her annoyance at my mini-lecture. "I'll think about giving it a chance."

I fight the urge to share my recent fear with Adrian. She'd be very supportive and help me find out for sure. There's just no way to keep Hamilton's name out of it. If I randomly hooked-up with any other guy, I would confide in my friend. Of course, she would poke and pry trying to get every little sexy detail out of me. Unlike her, I believe intimate details should remain between two people. I can't tell her the desperate favor I asked of our friend. She wouldn't be able to keep a Madison and Hamilton hook-up secret from the rest of our group. Since I can't tell her about Hamilton, I can't tell her how my fear grows exponentially with every passing day. I attempted to remain positive the past eight days, but I can't not know any longer.

TWENTY-EIGHT

Reasons for visits to the doctor or small local hospital are topics of gossip. HIPPA doesn't prevent sharing of this confidential information in a place like Athens. It's just one of the 4,724 reasons I want to escape this town.

Adrian: What are you doing today?
Me: chores around the house
Adrian: text me when you're done
Adrian: we'll plan something
Me: (thumbs up emoji)

I WANT nothing more than to hang with my friends today. Almost anything is preferred to what I must do. I pray I'm wrong. I hope I miscalculated or the stress of college this fall is the cause. I am not the type of person that can wait and see. I need to know. I must know, and the sooner the better.

I leave a note on the refrigerator, letting Memphis know I am running errands and to text me if she needs anything from town. It's not a lie. I just didn't say which town I would be in. I found online that a town west of Athens has a family-owned pharmacy. I plan to make my purchase there, hoping no one from Athens is around or works inside. It's far enough away they shouldn't know my mom, so that is good.

I blare my playlist through my car stereo the entire drive. I attempt to let the heavy beats and lyrics rescue my thoughts from my worries. I find that even Slipknot, Nine Inch Nails, Hailstorm, and Seether can't distract me today.

The outcome of this test will affect so many things. College this fall, my part-time job in Columbia, as well as the plans for the rest of my life. My future may change, but I will not let it affect Hamilton. If it isn't to affect him, that means I can't stay in Athens where his family and friends reside. *How can so much ride on the outcome of this little test? My favor of Hamilton may change the trajectory of my entire life.* I try to remind myself to not jump to any conclusions, but it is hard not to think of the worst possible outcome.

My heart rate speeds up when I park in the tiny parking lot. I take a moment in an attempt to work up the nerve to walk inside. I mentally tell myself to pull up my big girl panties and make my purchase.

Only two other vehicles populate the small lot. When inside, I realize they most likely belong to the pharmacist and the clerk at the register. The neat-as-a-pin pharmacy is void of customers. I am greeted by the clerk, informing me to be sure to ask if I have any questions. *Nope. There won't be any questions.* I pick up the major brand pregnancy test in its slim box and quickly approach the register in hopes of completing my transaction before any customers arrive.

"Will this be all for you?" the middle-aged woman at the register inquires. I simply nod, pay with my debit card, then graciously accept the white paper bag concealing the test. "Thank you and come again."

I breathe a sigh of relief when safely sitting behind the wheel of my car. My next step is a stop at the McDonald's on the edge of town. My bladder is anxiously awaiting its first visit to the restroom today. I found online that first morning urine is the best to test with early in a pregnancy. I slide the test from its box and slip it into my purse.

Safely tucked in a locked stall, I prepare to perform the test. I've never given much thought to peeing on a stick before. Turns out it isn't an easy task for a woman. Certainly not a graceful task to say the least. I recap the test, wrap it in tissue, and place it in my purse. I avoid looking in the mirror while I wash my hands. With little sleep last night and the fear of my test results, I am sure I look affright.

I set my cell phone alarm for two more minutes, assume the driver's seat in my car, and begin my journey back towards Athens. At the end of the longest minutes of my life, I peek at the result window. A pink plus sign ensures I am indeed pregnant with Hamilton's baby. Tears well in my eyes, and my hands tremble on the steering wheel. I swerve dangerously at the last minute onto a gravel road. When I throw my car into park, my chest tightens, and I struggle to pull in a breath. I should have known not to read the test while driving sixty miles per hour down the highway.

I allow myself several minutes to cry, to feel sorry for myself, and to overreact. Then, I wipe away my tears, take several deep breaths, and shake my hands out. I pull out my cell phone and start to plan, making a list.

First, I should contact my college advisor, Odessa, to see what options I still have for the year. Next, I should buy a pregnancy book to ensure I do everything I can to have a healthy baby. I should research towns to relocate to in case I cannot attend college this fall. The last note I type on my digital list is to schedule an obstetrics appointment far away from Athens.

Calmer now with a plan in place and certainty to my status, I continue my drive home. I opt to listen to the local radio station, turned low, as my mind needs no further distractions. Although my thoughts should be one-hundred percent on the road, I realize my summer plans will change now, too. I'll need to pack meals when I am working away from the house, I'll need to limit my time in the hot sun, and I should give up caffeine immediately. This seals my duty as the designated driver, not that I ever really drank alcohol.

I wish I had a close friend to share my secret with. Hamilton would be that person, but this is one secret I can't share with him. He would quit baseball and take over his mother's farm the very day I told him. He'd abandon his lifelong dream, the dream his father talked so proudly of. It was never assumed he would take over the farm. They hoped he would attend college and play baseball as long as he could. I can't let the favor I asked of Hamilton change his life and the hopes of his parents.

Still driving, I silently hope I don't start to show before I leave for college or am able to move from Athens. Perhaps I should attempt to move up my departure.

Back in Athens, I stop at the grocery store to pick up the items I know I need to purchase. I say hi to a few people in the store, my secret weighing heavy in my thoughts.

"You need more cereal," Savannah's voice informs as my cart rolls by her stocking the grocery shelves.

"Not that kind of cereal," I state as she attempts to place two boxes in my cart. We chat for a few minutes before I excuse myself to let her get back to work.

I feel guilty that I can't share with her or any of my girlfriends. They won't understand my not wanting Hamilton to give up everything to take care of me. They would fill my thoughts with the idea of moving to Des Moines to be with him. But I know him better than they do. He wouldn't be able to give one-hundred percent to baseball if we were there, and he wouldn't be able to give one-hundred percent to me and the baby while playing baseball. That would not sit well with him. He would drop everything and move back to Athens where he knew he would be able to support us easily. One of us may have to give up our dream of escaping Athens, but I won't allow both of us.

TWENTY-NINE

Back-to-school supplies are only available at the grocery store and the farm supply store—that's another of the 4,724 reasons I want to escape this town.

I NERVOUSLY FLIP through a random magazine as I wait to meet with my advisor. I desperately still wanted to attend college this year, so I reached out to her via email, explaining the change in my situation. I pleaded with her to discuss options that might allow me to still attend classes while pregnant and later with a newborn. She scheduled this meeting without explaining if options existed. Thus, I nervously wait to hear if I can indeed leave Athens for college, or if I will have to move somewhere else.

"Your advisor will see you now." The receptionist informs.

I rise and enter her office.

"Hello, Madison, I'm Odessa." She motions to the two chairs facing her desk. "Please make yourself comfortable."

She moves several papers and file folders from in front of her to the credenza at her back. Placing her elbows on the cleared desktop, she leans towards me, a smile upon her face.

"I am glad you emailed me about the change in your situation," Odessa begins. "How have you been feeling?"

I don't want idle chit-chat. I want to know if the life I planned is still an option. I want to demand answers but know I must be courteous. "I feel good; nervous, anxious, scared, but no morning sickness yet."

She nods, selects a paper from the stack in her wire basket, and places it before her on the desk. "Let's see what we can do to ease your mind. Pregnant students are permitted to live in the dormitories. Those who marry choose to reside in married housing or off campus. The university will still honor all scholarships and dorm assignments for you this fall and spring until you deliver the baby. Children are not allowed in the dorms. You will need to find other accommodations at that time. Your academic scholarships will still be available for your studies."

I nod my understanding as a wave flows over me. I can still attend college. I still have a place to live this fall. I haven't messed my entire future up.

"Madison, I don't see you as the typical MU student. You arrive as a junior, not a freshman. Your previous coursework, grades, and CLEP testing demonstrate you will be an asset in our student body. In our two previous meetings, I feel I learned much about you, so I have another possibility for your housing." Odessa takes a sip of her coffee.

"An acquaintance of mine recently shared information about her family. I think we may be able to assist her, and she may be able to help us. My friend's father recently passed; her mother lives alone in the large family home, and all of the children reside out of state. She is contemplating placing her mother in a retirement community or moving her out of state. Her mother's name is Alma, and she's still active in the church and community. She is mobile, still drives, takes walks, and takes care of herself. The children are concerned she will be lonely and has no one nearby to keep an eye on her. I wonder if you might consider living in one of the four bedrooms, visit with her from time to time, and give the family peace of mind. She doesn't need a nurse, just someone near to check in with her occasionally."

My thoughts churn. I am not sure about this arrangement. Living off campus in a house beats a dorm room. There are many logistics to think of. I cannot afford to pay for my own meals, and my scholarships cover those on campus. I prepare to share my concerns when Odessa continues.

"I have arranged for us to have lunch with Alma today. I would like the two of you to meet prior to either of you agreeing to this arrangement. We should be going so we arrive prior to her."

ON THE RIDE, I recall all that Odessa shared in her office. I am not sure if I hope to live with Alma or in the dorm. I'm anxious to meet her to see if we are a good match.

As we make our way inside Murray's, we pass two teenage girls chatting with an older woman near the front door. They are discussing books they enjoyed reading this summer. One book they mention is the erotic romance I finished recently.

At our table, Odessa leans towards me. "Alma is in the group standing at the door."

I follow her pointing finger, to find the group discussing books. I now hope, since Alma and I enjoy the same types of books, maybe living together could work out. She can't be a stuffy, elderly woman if she openly speaks of erotic romance in public.

As we begin to nibble on our meal, Alma shares the story of how she met her husband on campus decades ago. I nearly spit my water across the table as she shares in detail the hot chemistry between them at the dance. It's as if I'm sitting across from an older version of Adrian. My fears lesson with her every word. I think this will be a good match.

"Odessa shared very little with me," Alma leans towards me from her side of the table and lowers her voice a bit. "Are you excited about your pregnancy? Do you plan to raise the baby?"

Just like Adrian, Alma holds nothing back. I sip my water as I search for the difficult answers. I decide honesty is important if I am to live with this stranger. "I didn't plan to become pregnant. Excited isn't the first word that comes to mind. Overwhelmed, scared, and stressed are a few of the feelings constantly swarming in my head." I take a deep breath in an attempt to open the tightness in my throat. "I didn't want to become pregnant at eighteen but finding myself in my current situation I *want* to keep our baby."

I scan surrounding tables to ensure other patrons are not listening to our conversation. "The father is my best friend. I plan to tell him about our baby later. He's chasing a dream, and I can't rip that away from him. I have no doubt he would drop everything and support us. One day in the future, I will give him that opportunity. For now, I plan to do the best I can on my own."

"What about your family? Memphis mentioned you are an only child, but what of your parents?" Instead of Adrian, Alma now resembles Memphis.

"I am an only child and my parents are only children." I fight the urge to rant negatively about my mother. Sometimes my rage outweighs my rational mind. "My dad passed when I was thirteen. My mother hasn't coped well since then. She struggles with depression and will not be helping me with the baby." If I live with Alma, I know I will need to share more about my relationship with my mother. In this moment it doesn't seem appropriate.

Alma places her wrinkled hand upon mine on the table. "From what I know of your academic ability and in meeting you today, I have no doubt you can handle this on your own until you are ready to let your friend in. I sense your fortitude. Although you haven't shared in detail, your eyes divulge you've experienced hardship. You have prevailed for eighteen years, you are a survivor."

Her words comfort. I desperately fight the tears pricking the back of my eyes and my sinuses. It's too early to blame them on pregnancy hormones. I deflect the topic from me. "Have you discussed a tenant with your family?" *Please take the bait. No more about my situation. It's too new and I haven't come to terms with every facet of it. I need time to adjust before I open my chest and share all of my secrets and fears.*

"My son, Trenton, attempts to assume the role as head of our family in these few months since my husband passed." Alma sighs while fiddling with her butter knife. "He doesn't like the idea of me remaining in my home alone. He coerces my daughters to urge me to move into an assisted living community." She chuckles. "That's just a fancy word for a nursing home. I don't need that. I'm healthy, active, and in control of all of my faculties. I know they worry about my living alone. My involvement in the church and community should be enough to ease their worries, but they are persistent."

Odessa excuses herself to the restroom. Alma slides closer to me. "I miss my husband. I love my home. It's full of memories of my babies and now my grandchildren. I can't box those up and take them with me. Every dent in the woodwork and scratch on the hardwood is a precious memory to me. I'll admit the house it much too large for one person. Heck, it's too big for two." She genuinely smiles at me. "I'm sure my oldest daughter, Taylor, reached out to Odessa. They went to high school together. When Odessa mentioned the opportunity for me to help a promising scholar attain her degree, I saw it as a solution to continue living the life I love while sharing my love with another."

"My children may not like a stranger living in my home. Trenton will blow a gasket." She smiles fondly thinking of the son. "He only means to protect me, but I'm about to remind him of his place in our family. I am his mother and he is my child. I'm sure the time will come when he will need to control my life, but I am not ready to give up just yet."

Her smirk is that of a defiant teenager. I fear Trenton is in for a long battle with his mother. I'm glad she continues to battle after the loss of her husband. I wish my mother had half of the strength I've witnessed in Alma today.

Before I know it, the check has been paid and Odessa announces she needs to return to campus. I love Alma. I can see myself living with her, spending time with her, and being happy.

"I would like to propose the two of you spend a couple of hours together at Alma's home today." Odessa's eyes dart between Alma and me. "Then, take a day or two to think it over before you let me know your decision." She flashes an encouraging smile our way.

Alma's eyes look to mine. "Madison, I would love to show you my home and visit this afternoon." I nod.

Odessa suggests Alma ride back to the office with us. Then, I can drive Alma home and leave from her house later this afternoon. I'm nervous for Alma to see my old car but realize I'm a college student; she expects me to drive an old car.

ALMA'S HOUSE is absolutely adorable. The two-story exterior is neat as a pin. I can tell it's been re-sided recently with fresh paint to the trim and shutters. The wrap around porch, complete with pillars and a porch swing, perfectly finish its curb appeal.

The interior is decorated with comfortable furnishings, family photos, and thriving house plants. Alma explains her bedroom moved into the back dining room a few years ago as the kids worried about their parents climbing the stairs each day. The kitchen is updated with stainless steel appliances and marble countertops. She seems to climb the stairs with ease. I understand why her children might worry but am glad to see Alma is indeed active.

She states that I would have my choice of the four bedrooms and three bathrooms if I choose to move in. The rooms are completely furnished with queen-size beds, dressers, bedside tables, lamps, and armoires. The color schemes are neutral, modern, and match the quilts that adorn the beds. One bathroom contains a glass-enclosed shower, the other a clawfoot tub with a tile shower stall in the corner. I know which bed and bathroom I will choose.

"Any questions about the house?" Alma asks as we return to the first floor.

"Alma, I want to be honest with you," I begin. "I enjoy your company, and I love the house." I like the soft smile my words bring to her face. "I only found out about the pregnancy last week. As I mentioned earlier, it's all new to me, and I'm scrambling to see if attending college is still an option for me."

Alma interrupts my confession. "Would you like a drink, maybe some water?"

"I'd love a water."

I join her in the kitchen. With water in hand, I continue at the kitchen island. "If I told the father about the baby, he would throw away his dreams and take care of me. I can't allow him to do that. I won't let him give up everything for me." I sip my water. "I already have enough credits, so I will be a junior this fall. I need only complete my final two years to graduate." I search my brain for anything else I should share.

She pats my hand upon the marble countertop. "Let's find a comfy chair, dear." I follow her back to the living room with water in my shaking hand. I really want this to work out. "I've shared my children's fears of my living alone so many miles away from them. I'm fortunate to be in excellent health. My husband left me financially secure. I enjoy shopping, dining out, going to movies, and attending church." She sighs. "By allowing a college student to move in, my children will gain peace of mind, I can continue living the life I love, and I receive a new friend. I've enjoyed our time together today. I want to offer you the opportunity to live with me while you attend college. I will not ask you to do chores or nurse me—I don't need that." She chuckles. "I have a cleaning lady visit twice a week. In exchange for room and board, I only need you to ease my children's worries. During our weekly calls, from time to time, you could say hello, and let them know all is good."

"Alma, I can't live here for free, and I can't let you buy my groceries."

"Madison, I am a mother and a grandmother. I love being a mother and as you will soon learn, you can't turn it off. Your living here will give me a purpose again. My late husband was a very successful surgeon. Trust that supplying meals for two instead of one will not inconvenience me." She smiles, morphing her voice from stern to calm. "We can cook together if you would like. The cost of remaining in my home is so much lower than the exorbitant amounts they charge to live in a retirement village."

I am grateful for the offer. With a baby on the way, not paying for meals would be helpful. A bubble of excitement swells in my belly. I really want to live here. I really want to help Alma by keeping her company. I know she will be helping me much more than I help her.

"If the offer still stands, I would love to live with you."

THIRTY

The fair parade is over an hour long, with more tractors and horse clubs than other floats—it's one of the 4,724 reasons I want to leave.

MEMPHIS AND ADRIAN join me at our spot along the fair parade route at 3:45. It's a humid, ninety-five-degree day. It will be a great night for the fair when the hot sun sets. We fan ourselves with a magazine while we wait, seated in our lawn chairs, in the outer part of the grocery store parking lot. Even this early, as we drove through town, most of the streets were lined, lawn chair to lawn chair, along the route. Kids sit, anxiously clutching plastic bags to fill with the candy that will be tossed from the floats.

Sometime after five, we hear the approach of police sirens signaling the parade is drawing near us. Adrian quickly connects FaceTime with Hamilton, like I promised we would, to include him in this tradition. He can't stay on long but gets a kick out of sharing it with his teammates.

Later the three of us walk around the midway for over an hour, often stopping to talk with people. The fair is a major event in Athens. Many people attend all six nights as well as an afternoon or two for the livestock competitions and other displays.

When we run into Salem, Latham, and Winston, Adrian joins their group for the rest of the evening. I'm sure Memphis and I will leave hours before she is ready to. The fair is not my thing. The carnival workers scare me, and it's like walking through a redneck convention. I smirk as Winston switches spots with Latham to walk beside Adrian. Their hands bump into each other a couple of times before the crowd envelops them.

It's my last evening in Athens. I am glad the fair distracts my friends as I slip away for the night.

THIRTY-ONE

The local radio station reads obituaries on the news daily—it's one of the 4,724 reasons I want to escape this town.

THIS DRIVE to Columbia isn't as exciting as first planned. It was to be Hamilton and I in his truck. Today, it's just me in my old car with a few boxes of clothes and things. The excitement I planned is replaced by fear. I planned to be on my own with one friend on campus; instead, I am responsible for a mini-human growing inside me. I planned to arrive the end of August—instead I'm starting my new life in late July.

I'm excited to live with Alma; we really hit it off, and I believe our arrangement will be mutually beneficial. I look forward to learning more about her family and the history of her house. She mentioned teaching me to cook, and I offered to help her with new technologies her children and grandchildren purchase for her. She'll teach me about my new town and help me not hide in my room. I'll ensure she stays active and safe for her family. She's nowhere near my age, but she assures me there are many students my age that attend her church and participate in activities there throughout the week.

I find, during my three hour drive, that my mind is free to contemplate many things. The guilt I feel for keeping my pregnancy a secret from Hamilton comes to mind. I regret not telling Memphis about our situation. She is an awesome mother and a great friend to me. I think she might have understood my desire not to share the pregnancy with Hamilton, but I didn't want to put her in a position to keep it from him. Then, the guilt for not opening up with Adrian floods my thoughts. Of my group of friends, she's the one that would have my back and hold my hair while I bent over the toilet with morning sickness. I only hope each of them will understand why I am keeping my pregnancy a secret for now. I realize I take the risk of losing them with my actions in this situation.

The cell phone Hamilton gave me is a blessing today as I use the Maps app for driving directions to Alma's home. When the voice alerts me that my destination is on the right, I find Alma sitting in her porch swing, smiling and waving as I pull in the driveway. As I exit my car, Alma makes her way to me.

"Welcome to your home away from home," she greets, pulling me into a hug. "Would you like to unload now or relax a bit?" She stands with her hands upon my shoulders.

"I could really use a restroom," I answer.

"Then we will unload after dinner," Alma states, guiding me up the steps into her home. "The restroom is second door on the left."

I nod and take my leave to relieve myself. While washing my hands, I look in the large mirror. I look the same as I did before I took the pregnancy test, met with my advisor, and plotted this new course. It hits me that I am officially in Columbia. I am officially starting my new life. I am equal parts scared and excited.

Upon joining Alma in the front room, I find she's prepared a tray with iced tea, cheese, and crackers. I join her on the sofa, gladly sipping the tea. Just as I prepare to start a conversation, the front door bell rings.

"Who could that be?" Alma looks to me before making her way across the room to peek through the curtain at the door. "What are you...?" She opens the heavy wooden door.

"Surprise!" What looks like a family of four shout.

Two little people wrap their arms around Alma while commenting on how they surprised grandma. She hugs the boys before greeting the man and woman, each holding a puppy.

"Who are these two adorable guys?" Alma asks while petting them both.

"Mom, may we come in?"

"Where are my manners?" she chides herself. "Madison, this is my son, Trenton, his wife Ava, and my grandchildren, Hale and Grant. Everyone, this is Madison." Alma explains I arrived only minutes before they did.

I exchange pleasantries with Alma's family. I feel I'm an intruder. My desire to move before August is interfering with her family plans. Trenton and his wife place the curly puppies down on the hardwood floor. Exploring the space, the two are so excited it appears their short little tails wag their entire back end. I join them on the floor. Immediately, two puppies take residency in my lap, lick my neck or face, and with paws on my shoulders, knock me backwards. As I lay on the floor, they continue to lavish licks as I laugh.

"Rescue her," Ava instructs Trenton.

He tucks one puppy under each arm while I return to my seat upon the sofa. Trenton explains they decided to take a family vacation to surprise Alma and meet me. I wonder if he really means to vet me. Alma seems surprised they are here. I'm sure her three children decided someone needed to meet me in person to ensure Alma's safety.

With our added guests, unloading my car takes little time at all.

I ENJOY Trenton's short two-day visit. Although I know he's here to check me out, I find him easy to talk to. His boys are absolutely adorable. As they play, I find myself imagining my little one as a boy playing games and talking baseball with his father, Hamilton.

As we eat dinner, I have to bite my lip not to giggle at them.

"You ask him," Grant whispers.

"No, you ask him," Hale whispers.

How the two boys think the four adults also seated at the table don't hear their whispers amazes me. Trenton tells his sons it's not polite to whisper at the table.

His oldest son, Hale, finds the nerve to speak up. "Dad, when can we tell Grandma?" Hale's eyes dart from his father to mother anxiously.

Trenton ruffles his son's hair. "Mom," he turns the conversation to Alma's side of the table. "One of the puppies is a gift from Hale and Grant for you." The boys preen. "When we visited the breeder, they couldn't choose between these two puppies. Hale, ever the negotiator, suggested we purchase both and let Grandma choose one, and we keep the other."

All eyes turn to Alma for her reaction. I pity the pressure her family just placed upon her. Not only would it be difficult to choose between the two adorable puppies, but her decision also decides which puppy her grandchildren get to keep. As Hale prefers one and Grant prefers another, it's like choosing one child over the other.

THE VISIT PASSES QUICKLY. As they pack up their gear, I assist Alma in preparing breakfast. We eat, say our goodbyes with promises to call soon, and they back out of the driveway on their way back home. Alma and I wave from her porch while Alma's new chocolate mini Labradoodle gnaws on his new leash in my hand. Of the two puppies, I am glad she chose the chocolate over the golden—he was my favorite, too.

Trenton's gift of a puppy is genius. A pet provides comfort and companionship while keeping Alma active. I smile to myself. Alma's son killed two birds with one stone this weekend. He vetted the strange college girl living with his mother, and he gifted Alma with another purpose to enjoy her life.

THIRTY-TWO

The grocery and farm store are the only places to purchase children's Halloween costumes. For variety or larger sizes, one must drive forty-minutes or shop online. This is one of the 4,724 reasons I want to escape this town.

WHILE ENJOYING a meal with Alma after church, my phone vibrates. It's a group text from Adrian.

Adrian: Video call 7pm tonight
Me: Yes, call my phone
Savannah: see you tonight
Salem: I can't wait
Bethany: will be there

PROMPTLY AT SEVEN, a video call from the girls rings my phone. The girls ask a million questions about my new room and the city of Columbia. I pull Alma into the video call for a bit to meet all of them. Later, I share about Trenton's visit, brag about Alma's adorable grandsons, and show them Alma's new puppy named McGee.

The girls chat about the latest gossip in Athens, the weather and crops, Adrian shares about her business, Savannah about the busy grocery store, then Salem and Bethany complain about their classes.

I miss my friends, and Columbia seems so far away. I know I wanted to get settled in before classes started, but I hate that I needed to leave weeks earlier than I originally planned. All too soon, we must end our call.

After much discussion, I relent and allow Alma to contact the obstetrics physician she and her late husband were close friends with. She assures me he is one of the best in the state. I worry about affording him, but she insists on taking care of that for me. I will not allow this. When I arrive at my first appointment, I will inform the doctor and his staff that I refuse to allow her to cover my medical expenses.

I find, in Alma's world of connections, things happen quickly at Alma's request. I'm anxious to learn if others quickly do her bidding out of fear or out of love for this caring woman. She called Dr. Anderson's office, and I have an appointment the next day. In a city as large as Columbia, this has to be unheard of. Even in Athens, we were lucky to get an appointment in two to three days' time. So, now I have little time to prepare myself for my first pregnancy appointment.

I've read the first few chapters in the pregnancy book Alma gave to me. It seems very comprehensive. Although it tells me what to expect on my first physician visit, I am still very nervous.

My nerves stem from my desire to be a great mom from the start. I worry that the changes I saw in my own mother after my father's passing might be genetic, affecting my ability to protect my baby. I want to be the mother I had in my childhood, but I worry things weren't the way I remember them. I'm nervous that my limited funds might not allow me to provide the best care possible. I also worry my bouts with depression may hinder my parenting.

As I am a single-mother, I am prepared for some to be unsupportive of my situation. I don't have to like it, but I've vowed to be strong. I fear that guilt will be the thorn in my side during my pregnancy. Although I know I am keeping my secret for the right reasons, I struggle with the guilt of not sharing with those I love.

Finally, thoughts of tomorrow's appointment fade and sleep finds me. As is my new routine, I wake twice to go to the bathroom and drink a glass of water. I find I am often very thirsty which, of course, leads to frequent trips to the restroom. It's a vicious cycle that I am sure I will endure the entire pregnancy.

THE NEXT MORNING, I wake after nine. I hear Alma's television on in the kitchen as I descend the stairs. The aroma of fresh-brewed coffee pulls me towards the kitchen. I've always loved the smell of coffee; I just haven't fallen in love with the taste. I'm lucky, because I would need to avoid it for the next several months if I did like it.

"I didn't start breakfast," Alma states as I enter. "Morning sickness can be harsh. Smells and tastes can set it off. I wanted to see how you felt first."

"Alma, you are so kind." Not only is she giving up a part of her house, but now she pauses her breakfast on my account. "So far, no signs of morning sickness. In fact, I'm starving." I look around the counters. "I think I'll fix some toast with peanut butter."

Alma enjoys her toast with jam. When she insists I didn't eat enough for breakfast, I promise to eat cereal in a couple of hours. She chuckles at my love of cereal. Apparently, she thought I was exaggerating when I told her I eat a bowl or two every day. It's actually my favorite snack.

An hour later, I am sitting beside Alma in the waiting room of the physician's office. Women in varying stages of pregnancy surround us. Some have a doting man with them, others have children in tow. I pat Alma's hand, glad I am not alone.

When my name is called, and I follow the petite nurse into the hall. She records my weight, takes my temperature, then escorts me to the exam room. I find the room much bigger than any room I've been in before. I'm instructed to fill a cup for my urine sample, remove all my clothes, and put on the gown with openings in the front. My situation just became very real to me.

As I sit on the crisp, crackling paper upon the exam table, I busy myself looking around the room. The posters on the wall share information on stages of pregnancy, location of the fetus moving through the birth canal, and even possible sleep positions for comfort. I ignore the metal utensils and tube of cream on the counter beside the sink. I notice many flyers filed on the side of a counter set at desk height.

A light rap at the door signals the doctor's entry. "Good morning, Madison, I'm Dr. Anderson and this is my nurse, Dawn." He makes his way to the stool at the desk and opens my chart on his tablet. Instead of reading my vitals or examining me, he sets the tablet down and rolls towards me. "You're a friend of Alma's. I'm so very glad she sent you my way. How do you like Columbia so far?"

This is not how I envisioned my appointment beginning. I explain Alma has taken me many places to shop, to walk, and to eat. I admit, I am looking forward to classes starting in about a month. He admits that Alma told him about my major and that I am starting as a junior instead of a freshman. He comments that I should consider medicine if learning comes easy to me, but admits teaching is a noble profession that is the backbone of all other careers.

Finally, he directs his attention to the reason for my visit. "So, you've taken a pregnancy test or two with a positive result. Let's get started." He sticks a strip in my urine that quickly gives him a positive pregnancy result. "Yep, very pregnant," he chuckles. "Can you tell me when you had your last period?"

"I can do better than that," I state. "I know the exact night I conceived."

He furrows his brow and explains it is very difficult to pinpoint the moment of conception. We usually count from the last day of the last period and use that as our base.

"I've only had sex once. It was the night of June Eighth. Well, I guess I had sex more than once that night, but that is the only date I've been with anyone." I shrug. "We used condoms, but since then I've read they are not one-hundred percent effective."

Dr. Anderson studies me for a minute to judge my honesty. "Alma shared some of your situation with me." He looks a bit embarrassed of his admission. "The father is not in the picture?"

"Oh, he would be if I told him. He got drafted by the Chicago Cubs. We were supposed to attend MU together this fall. He was to play baseball for the Tigers. Anyway, he got drafted, had 48 hours before he reported to their triple-A team in Des Moines, and I refuse to tell him about the pregnancy, because he will give up his dream of baseball to farm and care for me and the baby." I quickly swallow and continue rambling. "He's a good guy. The best. In fact, he's the perfect guy to have a family with. But I know how important his dream is. It was a dream he shared with his father before he died. I can't be the reason he gives up on his dream. So, I will attend school, have the baby, and a year or two down the road, when he is settled in Major League Baseball, I will tell him about our baby." Talk about diarrhea of the mouth—I'm out of breath.

Dr. Anderson looks to his nurse then back at me. "Not an easy situation to be in at the age of eighteen. Alma stated you have no family support either. I'm glad you have Alma with you during your pregnancy, but I am worried that you might need to tell others for additional help."

I know he only wants what is best for his patient and the baby, but I know my life situation better than anyone. I am doing the right thing for now. I can do this. With Alma's help, I will cope with the changes and stress of pregnancy and college and come out strong in the end.

Dr. Anderson, with the help of his nurse, complete my first

patient exam. We discuss prenatal vitamins, eating healthy, exercise, and other information I need to know about the upcoming appointment schedule. He tells me to call his office with any questions or if any unusual symptoms arise. He says his nurse will give me a print out of important numbers to call in case of emergency. Then, he says goodbye.

"Um, Dr. Anderson," I call. His nurse has already exited the room. "One more thing." I wring my hands in my lap. "I want to pay for my appointments myself. I don't want Alma to cover my medical bills. She is already doing me a big favor by sharing her house; it wouldn't be right for her to pay for my medical bills, too." *Not that I know how I will be able to pay for the bills*, I think to myself.

"I agree," he states, resuming his seat on the rolling stool. "But Alma isn't paying for your treatment. I am taking on your case pro-bono."

"I can't ask you to do that. Please, let me make payment arrangements," I attempt to argue.

"You didn't ask—I offered. I do research with the university. As an alumnus, I like to assist students when I can. From what I hear, you are an exceptional student. You will be one that MU can be proud of. I only want to help ensure you complete your education. For most appointments, I am only out my time. Occasionally, we will run a test that I will cover. All I ask in return is that you take care of yourself and your little one while you earn your degree."

I stare at him. *Is this guy for real? Who does this?* I shake my head. I am finding many people around Alma do these types of things. The blessing I thought I found in a place to live off campus is turning out to be a mega-blessing in disguise. I only hope I am able to repay the favors I am being given.

I SET my Mac on the dresser, open the webcam, and begin recording. I walk to the edge of the bed and take a seat. I ensure I see myself on the screen and begin.

"Today is August Eighth; I had my first obstetrics appointment with Dr. Anderson today. He assures me I am nine weeks pregnant. Both the baby and I are in good health. Thus far, we have no cause for concern. Well, he was a bit worried that I don't have a large support system, but I believe Alma and I will be able to handle this. I haven't gained any weight yet. I don't have any signs of morning sickness. I am tired all the time. I've learned I like naps, and if I didn't have to pee, I would sleep through the night." I pause, trying to think of anything else I wanted to share.

"Hamilton, you have a game tonight in Des Moines versus the New Orleans Baby Cakes. You're slated to be the starting pitcher." I lift the laptop to show the large schedule I have on the wall, the whiteboards with Hamilton's ERA and pitching rotation. "Alma joins the baby and I as we comb the internet for stats, pictures, and videos of you and the I-Cubs. I not only have ESPN app alert me and the baby of my favorite team, the Cardinals, but also the Cubs now, too. I hope I don't lose my Cardinals fan club membership for doing so. I've even set up Google alerts on the phone you gave me for the 'I-Cubs', 'Hamilton Armstrong+baseball', and 'Chicago Cubs+pitch.'" I return the laptop to the dresser. "That way, the three of us will know any news as soon as it goes public. It turns out your three biggest fans all live in Columbia, MO under one roof." I turn sideways in front of the webcam. "So, you can watch our little bundle grow..." I lift my T-shirt over my head. My abdomen is visible in my sports bra and low-waist shorts. "We are nine weeks pregnant. Our little baby is right in here." I point to my belly. "We love you and will post again soon." I walk over and stop the recording as tears well up in my eyes.

I want to create this visual journal for Hamilton. I want him to be able to see everything. I know my recording is no replacement for him helping me during the pregnancy, but he will be able to watch these videos and know we were thinking of him always. I hope in some small way, it will allow him to sort of experience our baby from the start.

THIRTY-THREE

The local radio station airs live interviews from the county fair. I don't need to hear how a fifteen-year-old boy raised his bull then won grand champion. Yet another of the 4,724 reasons I want to escape Athens.

I SIGN for a letter while Alma is fixing lunch. I see Taylor's name, Alma's oldest daughter, in the return address area. I assume it's our itinerary for the upcoming Chicago trip Alma's oldest daughter mentioned on our last call. Alma quickly opens the cardboard envelope to reveal our airline tickets for Thursday's flight. I quickly help Alma text Taylor to let her know we received the tickets before we enjoy our grilled cheese and chips. I'm actually looking forward to the trip. I've never been to Chicago. I know Taylor said we wouldn't do too much to wear out Alma, but I might try to slip away to do a bit of sight-seeing. During our light lunch, we plot our time to leave for St. Louis to ensure we have time for TSA before our flight. In my weather app, I share the Chicago forecast during our stay, so Alma and I will be prepared when we pack tonight and tomorrow. As I wash our lunch dishes my phone vibrates on the counter. It's a quick vibration, so I know it is an alert, not a text; I keep cleaning the dishes.

Later, I dry my hands then check for the alert that pinged my phone. The words cause me to drop my phone like it's on fire. I can't take a breath. I'm trying and trying; nothing is working. I bend over, lowering my head towards my legs. It takes everything I have to pull in short little puffs of air. I lean my hands on the counter, letting my head drop to the cold granite. The sensation calms me and helps me focus.

"Alma!" I scream. McGee runs toward me, barking.

She quickly comes to my side. "Madison, honey, what is it? Is it the baby?"

I can only shake my head and point to the ESPN alert on my phone screen. She reads it out loud. "The Chicago Cubs call up left-handed pitcher, Hamilton Armstrong, from their AAA team."

I witness the light bulb moment when the words compute for Alma. Her eyebrows rise sharply, eyes open wide, and jaw drops straight down. I nod my head in agreement. Although we speak no words, we agree this is freaking awesome. Alma breaks from the shock before me. She calms McGee with a dog treat before fetching a bottle of water. She removes the cap and urges me to sip while she rubs my back in a circular motion. McGee, still concerned, lies on my feet.

"He did it," I whisper. "In two months, he moved from the triple-A ball team to the Major League." I shake my head. "I knew he would, but now that he did, I can't believe it."

"This means we can watch his games live on television instead of constantly refreshing the computer browser to update the games stats."

This is why I've grown to love Alma. She quickly shared in my excitement of all things baseball and following Hamilton's stats. "We'll get the MLB package, so we can see all of his games."

I pick up my phone to shoot a text to the man himself.

Me: Just read the ESPN alert
Me: had mini heart attack
Me: I am so proud of you
Me: Congrats! You're in the big leagues
Me: I'm sure you're swamped today
Me: Just know we are celebrating down here in Columbia

NEXT, I call Memphis. "Are you sitting down?" I ask immediately. When she confirms, I share the news. "I'm not sure if Hamilton will have time to call you today, so I wanted to tell you. I just saw on ESPN that the Cubs called Hamilton up to Chicago today!" After my squeal, I give her time to have a mini-panic attack like I did.

"Madison!" I know she is struggling for words just like me. "I'm so proud of him. I guess you were right all along. You said he'd play in the Major Leagues. I never had the conviction you did. Thank you for being such a big fan and friend to him all these years." We chat for a bit before she lets me go to call her daughter.

I don't hear back from Hamilton until after ten p.m.

Hamilton: Are you awake?
Me: Yes!

I ANSWER MY RINGING PHONE.

"Can you believe this?" Hamilton begins. "You would not believe everything I had to do today."

"I want to hear everything!" I feel disconnected from him at this distance. I long to experience everything with him—I am his number one fan after all.

Hamilton shares the details of his exciting day.

"Did they tell you when you might get your debut?" I can't believe I am seriously asking my best friend when he will pitch for the Chicago Cubs.

"I take the mound Sunday against the Brewers. I can't believe I get to say that. I will be pitching against the Milwaukee Brewers at Wrigley Field."

"That is so cool." I know my words sound lame. There are no words grand enough for this.

We talk for over an hour before I let him go, stating he needs to rest before practice tomorrow. We promise to talk again before his big day Sunday. I fall asleep with a happy heart for my friend and all he has accomplished. I can't wait for the world to see how great he is.

THIRTY-FOUR

In Athens, most students are related to several of their teachers, one of the 4,724 reasons I want to leave this town.

OUR FIRST EVENING in Chicago flies by. I enjoy meeting Taylor's husband and two pre-teen daughters. Their apartment is a huge, two floor home. Alma and I stay in a guest room on the lower level with the girls' rooms next door.

Taylor's daughters ask if they can 'do it now'. I can't wait to see what the *'it'* is they have for Alma. They jog into the kitchen and return with an envelope for Alma and one for me. We are urged to open them at the same time. As we pull the ticket from inside, they shout "Surprise!" in unison while hopping up and down.

I can't believe my eyes. In my hand, I hold a ticket to Sunday's Chicago Cubs game versus the Brewers. It's a ticket to Hamilton's MLB debut. Taylor's husband explains they are season ticket holders at Wrigley. They sweet-talked the couple with season tickets next to theirs for the extra two Sunday game tickets. All four adults will attend Sunday's afternoon game at Wrigley Field. I get to see Hamilton's debut live in person. I can't believe my luck. Alma appears as excited as I am.

Before Alma and I shut the light off for bed, I shoot an email to Hamilton's agent.

Dear Mr. Sheridan,
I have a surprise for Hamilton Armstrong and was wondering if I might ask for your help.
I will be attending Sunday's Cubs vs. Brewers game. Below, I have attached a copy of my ticket for the game. I wonder if there might be any way for me and the three attending with me to see Hamilton after the game. I realize his MLB debut will come with a lot of press and other obligations. We would just like a brief moment to surprise him and say hello.
Thank you for all you do for Hamilton.
Sincerely,
Madison Crocker

I SWIM in the atmosphere that is Wrigley Field. Our seats are three rows behind the Cubs dugout. Taylor's husband must pay a fortune for them each year. I enjoy every stress-filled moment of Hamilton's big debut. I marvel at his fire-bolt of a left arm, the precision with which he paints the corners of the plate at will, his instincts and knowledge of the game, and watching a few MLB players buckle at the knees with his curveball. It takes everything in me not to wave like a fan-girl as he returns to the dugout each inning. In the bottom of the sixth inning, the pitching coach approaches the mound and makes a change. I nudge Alma, standing to wave frantically at Hamilton. I call his name as he returns to the dugout. He wears a huge smile as he waves to the excited fans, cheering the end of his debut.

"Hamilton!" I hop up and down as I yell at him over and over, waving both my arms above my head.

His eyes scan in our direction. In the exact moment he recognizes me, I freeze with my hand still in the air, mid-wave. His smile grows warmer for me. He gives a tip of the bill of his ballcap to me as he disappears into the dugout below.

"I can't believe you really know him," Taylor's husband leans forward to address me. "He had a huge game today."

I nod. In the top of the eighth, Alma nudges my shoulder then points to the aisle. My eyes follow her finger to find an event staff member asking for Madison Crocker. I carefully make my way to the aisle. I smile at his words.

I ask Alma to get Taylor's attention. "Want to go with me to see Hamilton?"

Alma and her family excitedly follow me.

We are escorted from the stands to an under the stadium hallway where Nelson Sheridan waits for us. I introduce Alma and her family. Mr. Sheridan ushers us to a small conference room where he asks us to wait for Hamilton after the game. Taylor and her spouse quickly take a selfie to brag about seeing private parts of Wrigley today. As the game plays on a mounted TV, we watch the Cubs claim the victory.

Waiting sucks. The anticipation of seeing Hamilton in person seems more than I can bear. This will be the first time I've been in his presence since learning I'm carrying his child. As our door is barely cracked open, we hear the press fill the hallway outside the locker room. It is announced that the pressroom doors are open. The excited throng exits the hallway, and the noise level greatly decreases. Mr. Sheridan pops his head in to state that Hamilton will be here in a moment.

I feel my belly flip-flop when Hamilton enters our room. His agent quickly closes the door, allowing us privacy for a moment. I am scooped into a tight embrace. Hamilton buries his head in my neck and hair.

"I can't believe you're really here," he murmurs. His hot breath on my ear prickles my skin and brings back memories of our night together. As he pulls away, we grin like fools. "Alma, it's nice to meet you in person."

"I'm glad to meet the man behind the stats we've reverently followed online." Alma shakes his hand. She introduces Hamilton to her family. He signs the back of all of our tickets, claiming they are his first four autographs as a Chicago Cub.

We congratulate him on his great outing today. He tries to put into words the moment his name was announced and when he first took the mound. He confesses he is nervous for the post-game press conference he will be leaving us for in a moment. Our time in his presence is brief, and I wouldn't trade it for all the gold in the world.

Once back at Taylor's home, I excuse myself for a bit. I record today's video journal entry by proudly displaying my ticket with Hamilton's signature from the game. I state that today was our baby's first time attending one of Daddy's games. I share Hamilton's comments about the crowd, the atmosphere, and his stats for today's game. I apologize on camera for keeping my secret, share that his talent for the game is the reason, and vow in the future, I will tell him everything.

THIRTY-FIVE

There is only one small shoe store in Athens, and it doesn't carry sports shoes. To get sports gear and shoes, you must order online or drive over forty minutes to the closest store. This is one of the 4,724 reasons I want to escape this town.

BACK FROM CHICAGO, Adrian asks me, via text, to call her as soon as I get unpacked. When I call, she excitedly shares how my seven friends in Athens watched Hamilton's Cubs debut.

"Two part-time employees volunteered to run the concession stand. Troy and Latham planned to start the projectors in all three theaters during the pre-game show to ensure all attending viewed the entire game. Bethany and Savannah offered to take tickets outside the outer door to help with the flow of the crowd. With all this help, Winston and I were free to float as needed and to welcome everyone."

"Wow!" If I wasn't in Chicago, I would have joined you."

Adrian beams. "I wish you could have seen Winston and his

parents' surprise when I announced tickets sold out in less than twenty-four hours. We raised $750 from ticket sales for the Athens Ball Association. Our community support for Hamilton's Major League debut was overwhelming. The entire $5 ticket price for the viewing was all donated to youth baseball and softball programs in Athens. The concession stand offered drinks and popcorn. All funds collected from food were also donated."

"Winston's family loved my idea to share Hamilton's debut as a local fundraising opportunity. I was so happy that I was able to help Winston in return for his assisting with my store."

"Before we began the viewing in each theater, Winston welcomed and thanked each group and reminded them the concession stand was open the entire game and all money would be donated. As each theater applauded, Troy and Latham started their projector."

"Winston invited Troy, Latham, Bethany, and Savannah to watch the game with us in his office. We took turns checking on all areas while the Cubs were at bat."

"In addition to the $750 we raised in ticket sales, we made $1250 in concessions and the free-will donation tubs. Athens truly came through on Hamilton's big day. They supported Hamilton in his debut and our local ball programs. Winston posted the total raised on the theater's Facebook page that night, and the community's comments were awesome. You should pull them up to read."

Sensing the end of her story, I can finally speak. "Adrian, that is awesome. You need to text Hamilton to call you when he can and share this with him. He will love this. Not only that Athens watched his debut, but donated money to help baseball and softball to do it." I am so proud of her.

"It's surreal that our friend is pitching in the Major Leagues. I am so happy you were able to be at Wrigley."

"I hope Winston rewarded you for all the planning you did on this. I'm sure it doubled as positive publicity for his theaters."

"I have no complaints," she giggles.

I'm so glad she's found Winston. I worried for so long that her need to be in control would prevent her from finding love in the small town of Athens. Although I am shocked that Winston allows her to lead at times, I am happy he does. My friend deserves happiness and he provides that for her.

THIRTY-SIX

There is only one dentist in Athens. For an orthodontist, you must drive twenty minutes, and he's only available two days a month. This is one of the 4,724 reasons I want to escape this town.

THE NEXT WEEK, Adrian calls me. I love that she still reaches out to me for advice or to brag about her encounters with Winston.

"Hi Adrian," I greet. "I hope you have a juicy sex story to share with your lonely, much-too-busy-to-date friend in Columbia."

"I did it again," Adrian confesses.

"Don't you mean, 'Oops I did it again'?"

"Nice one," she responds. "Madison be serious. In my haze, I even suggested we start dating like a real couple." She waits nervously for my reaction.

"Oh, Adrian, I am so proud of you. You should date him. Winston likes you a lot. And I could see while working at the store with you that you are smitten by him."

"Smitten? What the heck? I am not smitten. I don't lose control to be smitten. This isn't the 1960s. People don't get smitten. I don't know what to do. Help me please." She sounds frantic.

"Adrian, dating Winston is a good thing. It's okay to be nervous and scared. That means your feelings are new and genuine. Tell me what happened the last night, so I can help you."

"Winston texted me to come help him cover at the theater last night when I closed the store."

He ties her up in knots, and while Adrian fights her inability to control her reaction to him. She refuses to follow my advice to give the poor guy a chance and start dating.

"I recently realized I love the theater. The popcorn smell, the excited ticket purchasers, the red velvet seats, and curtains feel like home to me."

I desperately want to mention to her that it feels like home because Winston is there. She's not ready to hear that—she's getting closer but isn't quite there yet.

"I sold tickets while Winston covered the concession stand. I'm glad I don't hire part-time teenagers. They seem to be very unreliable."

"Adrian." I interject. Technically, we're still teenagers." We are only eighteen; we have two more teen years left. "I do understand what you mean, though."

"Winston asked me to keep him company until he closed. I nodded and asked what I could do to help. He simply flashed his sexy smirk, causing my body to hum, and walked me towards the office where we spent most of the next hour."

When Adrian pauses, I assume she means to signal they had sex in his office. "Tell me you didn't. Adrian, in his office?"

"No!" Adrian admonishes me. "Please, even I can restrain myself while at his work. Winston entered the ticket sales information into the computer, counted my sales drawer, and placed the cash in the safe. We talked about my day at the store and his visit with Troy. He described three pieces of furniture Troy has ready for me."

"I'm glad Troy is able to sell his work in your store. He has a great eye. Where I see a beat up old dresser missing a drawer, he sees a piece to repurpose." Although I pin many of these projects on Pinterest, I could never tackle such a project. "When I get my own place, I plan to buy several of his pieces."

"Cool. Now, stop distracting me. I'm getting to the important part, so listen up."

Adrian needs to get the entire story off her chest so I can help her. I attempt to bite my tongue until she spills the detail-laden story.

"Winston informed me we were going for a ride after he locked up. I paused at the passenger door of his truck to let him know I'm not the type of girl he can order around. Before I could speak, Winston leaned close and whispered he'd wanted to do *this* all night. I had no time to ask what he meant. His lips connected with mine. His kiss was needy, as our lips melded together. I mean, I was left a panting, leaning on his truck."

"He unlocked the passenger door and reached behind me to open it. Then, he had the nerve to take advantage of my position, climbing into his truck, and swatted my butt."

"He didn't."

"Not only that, but he closed my door and slowly strode to his side, wearing his sexy smirk. Then, with a shrug, he said he wanted to bite or swat my butt, and I was just lucky that swatting won out. I mean, who does that?"

I don't answer but want to tell her it sounds like something she would do.

"As he drove, I found I didn't care where we were going. I liked the last time he took me for a ride in his pickup. We returned to the same old farmhouse we visited before. We exited the truck, Winston lowered his tailgate, and I hopped upon it." Adrian's words are thick with emotion as she recalls last night.

I remember the feeling. Hamilton opened me up to feelings and pleasures I didn't understand in Adrian's previous stories. Now, when she briefs me on her escapades, I am very aware of the sensations and reactions she speaks of.

Done with the intimate details, Adrian shakes her head as she continues. "Then, I experienced diarrhea of the mouth. I blurted I'd be up for seeing where this thing goes."

"What was Winston's reaction?"

"I think his words were, 'Seriously? You mean if I had asked you out on a date you would have considered saying yes?' To which I asked if he wanted to ask me out before. Winston admitted a couple of times in the last year or so, he entertained the idea of asking me out."

"When I asked why he didn't, he said, and I quote, 'Adrian, you've got to know you kinda do what you want and say what you want anytime you want. I figured if I interested you, you'd have let me know.' I informed him I did tell him I thought he was hot before."

"He then had the balls to respond, 'You did, but I'm not sure if you are aware of it or not; you tend to state a lot of guys are hot. I wasn't sure if you meant anything by it.' Can you believe this guy?"

I don't dare answer her. She's on a roll. She has a story to finish.

"So, I informed him we're trying it now. No reason to discuss any time we wasted. I asked when he would take me on our first date."

"Placing his index finger on my chest, he said I needed to plan to take him on a first date. He tells me I will take him on our first date. Madison, how do I react to this?"

I choose my words carefully. I need to coax Adrian in to doing what she wants but fears. "First, Winston is a unicorn. You need to claim him before someone else reaps what he provides." My words make her laugh. "Seriously, Adrian, you state you feel very different, and you lose control with him. Your body and your mind want Winston. I know it scares you, but you feel more alive when he's near, right?"

"Yes." Her voice sounds small. "I feel weak, and I don't like that."

"Do you feel weak, or do you lose control?"

She ponders my question. "I lose control. The things he does, the way he makes me feel, I just..."

"It's primal," I explain. "Your body takes over, your mind shuts down, and you just feel. That's not weak. It's actually the opposite. You're letting your body and his body give you pleasure. You're still in control. You know what feels good, you know what you like, and you know what to do. You are still in control. He's not taking your control away. He's opening you up to feel, to love. I love this. Winston is *good*. He knows you well enough to know you like to be in control. I think he'll have staying power." I smile. loving Winston's effect on my friend.

"Easy. We've only agreed to one date to see how it goes. Don't start talking about staying power. We're not planning to marry."

"So, when and where are you taking him on your first date?"

"That's where I need your help."

"You don't need my help. You know what he likes. You know what you like. Just plan something simple."

"You're no help."

"You should cook for him. You could putt with him on the practice green at his golf course. Allow him to teach you proper putting techniques. Guys like to teach girls. Watch the sunset from the dock at the lake or park on top of a hill." I pause to think. "Oh, I know. After dark, park somewhere quiet. Spread thick blankets and pillows in the bed of his truck. Then, watch a movie on a laptop or iPad. It would be your own private drive-in movie."

"I like that one," Adrian admits. "I knew you were the girl to ask for advice. Thank you. I need to let you go now so I can start planning it all."

"Eager much? You could wait to take him on a date tomorrow night."

"Duh," she quips. "I need to give him notice so his parents can cover at the theaters. Now that I know what I want to do, I'm going to call him, so we can plan when to do it."

"Text me the details. Then text me after the date."

"Got to go! Bye!"

THIRTY-SEVEN

The nearest furniture store is forty minutes away. Only used furniture is available in Athens. This is one of the 4,724 reasons I want to escape this town.

"HEY MADISON," Adrian greets when our FaceTime connects near the end of September. "How's college life treating you?"

"I love my methods classes. The professors are cool. How's everything in Athens?" I wonder if the camera angle shows I've put on a little weight. It might only be five pounds, but I see changes in my face and stomach already.

Adrian jumps right in. "I get to go first; my news is juicy." She wiggles her eyebrows up and down. "I am officially dating Winston."

I puff up like a peacock. I'm proud that Adrian listened to me during our phone calls and recent texting sessions. I encouraged her to take a chance. She never would have without my encouragement.

"Hey, where is Savannah?"

Salem answers before Adrian can. "It's deer season, silly," she giggles. "You know how much Savannah enjoys bow hunting this time of year."

"Before you groan, we know. Deer season in Athens seems like a holiday, and it's one of the reasons you couldn't wait to leave Athens." Adrian attempts to sound like me when I complain about their little town. They've heard my complaints a million times.

"You forgot to complain about the disgusting deer carcasses hanging from trees in peoples' front yards during deer season," Bethany adds, and I groan loudly.

"And last but not least, she hates how half the grocery store parking lot doubles as the deer check-in station where people hang out and compare racks in the back of their trucks." Salem adds.

"Nice guys, real nice," I admonish. "Let's just say, I am not missing any part of deer season this year."

"So, you aren't curious to see if the guys have a deer yet?" Adrian asks.

I remind them Savannah's the only one that participates in archery season. Since she's missing the call, she must not have one yet. Since the guys only go during gun season, they don't have theirs yet either.

Our call tonight is shorter than usual. I claim I need to read chapters for tomorrow's classes, but I'm exhausted. The first trimester of pregnancy is taking its toll on me.

SEVERAL DAYS LATER, Adrian calls as soon as I am home from classes. She shares that they've developed a new couples habit. Winston tends to bring her lunch at the store, and she takes him dinner at the theater.

"So, last night, I grabbed a pizza and spent the evening keeping him company in his office. I enjoy the nights all the part-timers show up for their shifts, letting us chill in the office instead of covering their shifts."

"I announced I had an idea after we enjoyed a few bites of our meal. I told Winston he should hire an assistant manager to allow him a couple of nights off each week. He didn't respond while he pondered my words. Then, he smiled and motioned for me to join him on the other side of his desk. He pulled me onto his lap."

"We discussed hiring an assistant means we could enjoy evenings together, go on real dates, and attend parties. I was relieved he liked the idea immediately. I had planned to convince him, so I decided to push my luck and share my other idea."

"I rose from his lap and closed his office door. When I turned back, Winston's blue eyes were liquid, and his lips quirked up on one corner in a devilish smirk. I licked my lips while I stepped closer to him, explaining I had an even better idea I wanted to share with him."

Winston got the wrong idea. He said, 'While I want nothing more... we really should act responsibly while I am at work.'"

"I stated while I loved where his mind went, that was not what I wanted to share. I mentioned one of us should get an apartment. I explained it would be nice to spend an evening together that isn't in our parents' house."

"He added we wouldn't need to use his truck to park in the country either."

"We spent the rest of the night discussing rentals: where we could find one, who to call, and how nice it would be to have alone time there. We pulled a few listings up on the internet. Of the five we found, two were cute little houses. So, I think we will be looking at rentals later today and tomorrow. Winston liked the idea so much, he's eager to move forward as soon as possible."

I share in Adrian's excitement as we discuss all the good points of a place of his or her own. I'm glad she is enjoying her time with Winston instead of fighting her feelings. I share a bit about my classes, assignments, and the Bible study I enjoy each week at Alma's church before we say goodbye.

THE NEXT MONDAY NIGHT, Adrian texts me a photo of a house. Her text claims Winston decided to buy this house instead of rent. This news is much too big to be texting about.

I dial her phone. Adrian shares how he surprised her by blindfolding her as he drove her to the house. She explains as he gave her a tour, he mentioned how each room reminded him of her and that it had plenty of room for their future children.

Of course, I have to calm her worries that he is moving too fast. We discuss that he bought the house; they didn't buy it together. He plans to move in and didn't mention the two of them living together yet. I'm sure it's the mention of their future children that causes her concern. I know she is eager to run her business, marry, and start a family, but she is scared of the feelings Winston gives her.

We chat for more than an hour. Before I feel she is in a good place, and I can let her go.

TWO MONTHS LATER, I'm counting down the minutes until my call with the girls. Adrian claims to have good news to share with all of us.

"Hello girls," I greet when the video call connects with my phone. I take great care to only frame my face in the camera view. At five months pregnant, my body is beginning to show my added weight.

Adrian is not visible on my screen. She's usually up front in the center.

"We have been dying to call you for three hours now," Salem states.

She explains. "Adrian texted us this afternoon that she had a juicy secret to share on the video call tonight," Savannah informs.

"She wouldn't give us hints or let us call you early either," Bethany fake pouts.

"So, where is Miss Adrian with this juicy secret?"

At my question, Adrian appears behind the three girls. She doesn't speak; she simply slips her left arm through the girls and wiggles her ring finger.

"No way!" I scream.

Savannah, Salem, and Bethany swarm the diamond then wrap Adrian in a tight group hug. As the celebration calms, Adrian assume her usual position in front of the webcam.

She shares in great detail how Winston proposed last night while recreating the drive-in movie date we concocted for their first real date months ago. A permanent smile graces her face.

"We're planning a May wedding. Oh, and Madison, will you be my maid-of-honor?"

I'm sure my eyes are the size of saucers. I quickly calculate the time from my due date to a May wedding. I might have lost most of my pregnancy weight by then.

"I will be honored to be your maid-of-honor," I inform my friend.

"Madison gets to plan the bachelorette party!" Bethany squeals.

"Adrian, you'll need to call me, so we can start planning," I state.

Later, as we say goodbye, I'm sad I'm not there to celebrate with them. I wish I could have driven up to share news in person. I must continue to hide my secret, so I pretend my schedule doesn't match theirs anytime they invite me up. This is my sacrifice. For my little one and for Hamilton, I can hide here in Columbia. My classes and homework keep me very busy. The visits each week with the girls keep them in my life. Although I regret my slow withdrawal from them, I must think of my future and of my baby.

THIRTY-EIGHT

Clothing must be purchased at a Walmart a few towns away, in a city an hour away, or online. Just another of the 4,724 reasons I want to escape this town.

IT'S MARCH, and I'm gigantic. I spend most of the day horizontal on the sofa before turning in early to bed. I slide from the sofa with the grace of an elephant. Slowly, I waddle towards the restroom. The urge to pee grows with each step.

"Alma!" I call. When she peeks into the hallway from the kitchen where she is fixing dinner, I inform her I just peed myself.

As she nears, Alma states it's not urine—my water broke. She turns me towards the front door. "Go! I'll meet you in the van."

As I waddle, she quickly grabs our purses and my overnight bag. I make my way to the porch, down the steps, toward her car. As I open the passenger door, I remember the dog. *McGee!* I mention to Alma he is still in the backyard. She quickly places him in his kennel before joining me in her car.

I don't hear anything she says during the drive. I'm sure she is attempting to calm my nerves. I can only worry about the upcoming pain and the fact that Alma is the only one with me for the delivery.

Once at the hospital, I'm whisked to the obstetrics ward with Alma by my side. Alma's phone vibrates often, and she replies to each text. I know she is letting her children know we are at the hospital. They've called and texted me every day for the past two weeks to offer words of encouragement or distract me from my constant need to rest.

Nurses scurry around; I'm in a gown, on a bed, with monitors upon my belly within minutes. I'm told Dr. Anderson will arrive in moments, and I should rest as much as I can before the labor progresses and the baby arrives. How am I supposed to rest with the loud fetal monitor? The baby's rapid heartbeat drums from the speaker. It calms my nerves. My baby is safe, and soon, I will hold him or her in my arms.

Dr. Anderson informs me that my water did indeed break, and, although I don't feel any labor pains yet, they will be arriving soon. Again, I am encouraged to rest while I can.

The next knock at the door brings Alma's daughter Taylor into my room. "Surprise!" She places a kiss on my cheek and squeezes my hand. "You didn't think I would miss the big day, did you?"

In my confusion, I cannot reply.

"I made plans to visit after your last appointment. Imagine my surprise when mom texted that your water broke, and you were on your way to the hospital; I was already driving to Columbia when I got the message." She chuckles. "We timed it perfectly. Now, do you mind if I am in the room while you are in labor? Or would you prefer I wait in the other room?"

"Stay," I beg as I clutch her forearm. "Please stay." my voice quivers, advertising my fear to both of them.

"I need to ask a favor." She purses her lips. "The girls would like a picture of you before and after the baby arrives." She quickly continues before I refuse. "Trust me, I told them no one wants a picture while they are in labor. But, you know my girls; they are the selfie queens."

"Let's take a selfie before I start screaming and sweating."

Alma and Taylor lean in while Taylor snaps the picture. She shows it to me for my approval prior to sending it to the girls. She tells me how the girls begged to be taken out of school and be here for the birth. I smile at their antics.

I quickly record a video for Hamilton, explaining where and when my water broke, that Alma drove me to the hospital, and Taylor met us here to surprise me. I include Alma and Taylor in the video. They smile, wave, and promise to take good care of me.

Soon, my labor pains begin. Although the nurses claim these are mild contractions, I find them unpleasant. If these are mild, I am not sure I will survive natural childbirth. Suddenly, a C-section sounds like a good idea to me.

I find I slide in and out of sleep between contractions. When Alma excuses herself to find some coffee and breakfast, I realize morning has arrived.

"Taylor." She hops from the chair in the corner to my bedside. "Will you record me for a minute?" She gladly takes my phone and tells me to begin.

"Hi Hamilton," I greet. "Hours have passed. As you can tell by my appearance, the labor pains are taking their toll on me. On his last check, Dr. Anderson claimed I am progressing nicely. He predicts our baby will arrive later today. I hope he is right. Delivering on March Tenth sounds much better to me than labor continuing until March Eleventh. Although I wish you could be here, I'm glad you aren't. I can't control myself when a contraction occurs. I'm verbally abusing Alma and Taylor. I'll never be able to make this up to them."

I pause as a contraction begins. "Keep recording," I instruct through gritted teeth.

"Remember to breathe," Taylor prompts.

"I am breathing. I'd be dead if I didn't...UHH!"

Alma returns. She quickly places a cold cloth upon my brow and whispers calming words into my ear. She talks of baseball, Hamilton pitching, and watching the games this season with a little baby on our laps. She promises to buy tiny Cubs attire for Hamilton's newest fan. Her words help me through the pain.

I take a couple deep breaths before looking back at the camera. "As you can see, you are missing all the fun here. This will probably be my last post until our little one makes its way into the world. I am looking forward to finding out if we have a son or a daughter very soon. We love you." I signal for Taylor to end the recording as the next contraction hits me.

"I CAN'T BELIEVE you allowed Taylor to record the birth," Cameron, Alma's youngest daughter, states. I laugh at the FaceTime screen as Alma holds her phone. "Trust me, I don't want to see it. EVER."

"I made her stay above my waistline. It just shows me in my supermodel delivery room face, the doctor announcing it's a baby girl, and me holding her for the first time." I kiss the top of my daughter's tiny, dark-hair-covered head and pink cap. "But, I won't force anyone to watch it. I recorded it for Hamilton."

Taylor extends her FaceTime call with her daughters toward me. "The girls want to know if you have chosen a name yet?"

I signal for Alma and Taylor to bring the cameras closer to my little one. "I'd like for you to meet Liberty Armstrong. Libby, this is your new family." I tickle her cheek with my index finger. Liberty yawns before placing her little fist in her mouth and sucking.

The loud reactions to her little movements through the phone startle her from her nap. Her eyes peek open over her chubby cheeks framed by her dark lashes moments before she begins to cry. Instant fear that I might not know how to calm my daughter floods over me. I tramp down my fear. I don't have time for doubt. I am her mother and I can do this. I tuck her tighter to my chest. I soothe her while Alma and Taylor end their calls across the room.

Once calm, I ask Taylor to record a message for me before we attempt to nap. "Hamilton, I would like to introduce you to your daughter, Liberty 'Libby' Armstrong. I opted for no middle name, so she may keep her maiden name when she marries. Stop. Breath." I imagine overprotective new dad Hamilton freaking out at the thought of his daughter dating, let alone getting married. I laugh into the camera.

"I know it will be two or three decades before she needs to worry about that. She weighs nine pounds and three ounces, is twenty-three inches long, and very healthy." I remove her little pink cap and brush her curly dark hair down. "She has her daddy's curls, brown hair, and appetite. She makes little piglet sounds as she nurses. We're both exhausted but wanted to say hi to you before we attempt to nap. We'll record more later tonight and tomorrow."

Alma places Libby in her bassinet then coaxes me to sleep while Taylor and she eat dinner. Food sounds good, but I'm too tired to eat right now. They shut off the light as they leave the room, and I quickly slide into slumber.

THIRTY-NINE

Athens has one small hardware store. For home improvements, you must drive over an hour away. This is one of the 4,724 reasons I want to escape this town.

THREE WEEKS PASS AS if only a day. Alma expertly assisted in creating a schedule at home. She insists I sleep when Liberty sleeps and takes care of everything around the house. Between nursing every three hours and completing my classes online, I don't have much time for anything else. Occasionally, Alma asks me to help her in the kitchen while Liberty swings nearby.

Tonight, is my weekly call with the girls. I still avoid video calls. As my hands are a doughy mess, Alma connects the call while holding a sleeping Liberty in her arms.

"Hello," Alma's voice greets. "I'm putting you on speaker as Madison is currently rolling cookie dough into balls for me."

"Good. I'm glad you are on the phone, Alma," Adrian begins. "I have a big announcement for all of you to hear at the same time. I'm pregnant!"

You could hear a pin drop for moments before Savannah laughs, Salem coughs, and I can only imagine Bethany's wide-eyed reaction.

"How did Winston react?" I ask. "Will you two get married right away?"

My questions catch Adrian off guard. She expected shock and comments about safe sex. Instead, I am calm and start to plan for her future. I know how pregnancy and the birth of a baby can change many things in their life, but she doesn't know about my own pregnancy experience.

"He was shocked and scared but supportive. We only found out yesterday, so we want to wait a day or two before we plan the future," Adrian states before seeking more of a reaction from the group. "C'mon you guys, where is my support? Say something."

She allows the conversation to continue for about five minutes before she jumps back in. "April Fools!"

Curse words and playful swats attack Adrian. Apparently, as her friends, we could see her being irresponsible in her relations with Winston. We inform her this is an April Fool's Day prank in very poor taste.

THE NEXT TUESDAY, Adrian calls me yet again for advice. She calls promptly at 1:00 p.m. as she knows I will be home from classes. I let the phone ring four times while I lay Libby in her bassinet before I answer.

"Hi," I greet, not pulling my eyes off the television.

"What's up?" Adrian nonchalantly asks.

"Seriously?" I ask in disbelief. "I'm watching Hamilton pitch—it's opening day. Please tell me you knew that."

"Sorry, I forgot. How's he doing?"

I share in great detail the changes in his stance and the increased strength in his arm this season. I tell her how many miles per hour each of his pitches gained during the off-season. Finally, I inform her he struck out all three batters he faced in the first inning, and they have two outs so far in the second inning.

"Can I just hang on until he gets another out, then we can chat while the Cubs bat?" She must really want to talk to me today. She waits patiently as I give her the pitch-by-pitch commentary to finish the half inning.

"Okay, I can focus now," I prompt.

"I need some advice. I know we talked about holding my bachelorette party the night before the wedding, but I want to really party and not be in bad shape on my wedding day. I mean, it is the first time you're coming back since August. We need to really celebrate. What do you think?"

I don't immediately answer. "I'm opening my calendar, so I'm putting you on speaker," I say as I move into the kitchen so as not to disturb my sleeping daughter. "The weekend before is Mother's Day, and I don't want to be in the same county with my mom then. So, it needs to be the first weekend in May." I pause, and she waits. "We could do it May Fifth. Salem graduates from her LPN program that day, and it's Cinco de Mayo, so it would be a great night to party. I had contemplated driving up for Salem's pinning; this would allow me to do it."

This is why she needed to call me today. I'm organized. I'm a planner. She knew her freaking out about moving the bachelorette party wouldn't be necessary if she asked me for advice. "You are AWESOME! This is why I love you. You can figure out and plan things so much easier than I can. Thank you. Thank you. Thank you." She makes kissing sounds in the phone for me.

"No problem," I reply. "Everything else falling into place? No 'bridezilla' moments or fights with the mother-of-the-bride?"

"No, all is calm here. Winston keeps worrying I will have a breakdown at any moment. I tease that he has seen too many movies. We're planning a casual wedding and reception. Easy-peasy."

I wish I were closer to help her with the plans, but Bethany and Salem have stepped up to help with items we discuss frequently over the phone.

"I'll send out the online e-vites for the bachelorette party after the game today. I'll probably just drive up the morning of the fifth. I'll ask Memphis if I can crash with her Saturday night, and I'll need to be back in Columbia before dinner on Sunday."

"Sounds great." She knows I want her to let me go so I can get back to Hamilton's game. "I'll let you get back to the game. Cheer loud for Hamilton for me. Bye."

FORTY

There are two mechanics in Athens. Yet another one of the 4,724 reasons I want to escape this town.

ADRIAN IS the first to arrive in the auditorium for Salem's pinning ceremony. So, she texts all of us where she is saving seats.

Though they attempt to keep their excitement and celebrating to a minimum, we get many stares as they welcome me when I arrive in the auditorium. They even fight a tear or two when I hug each friend. I've been away too long. It seems surreal that I will be in Athens twice this month.

My girls attempt to pry details of tonight's party from me. "All I'll say," I begin as all ears lean toward me eagerly, "is that we are meeting at Adrian's house at four this afternoon. You need to bring cash, debit cards, your ID, dress to impress, and bring a full change of comfy clothes for later." I only share what I've already put in the e-vite for the event.

We quiet as the ceremony begins. When Salem is announced, we whoop and cheer loudly to show we are proud of our friend. They keep the ceremony less than an hour long, and we congratulate She with her family afterwards. Salem asks us to wait for her while she says goodbye to them.

When she returns, she actually skips toward us. Her excitement with finishing her classes shines on her sun-kissed face.

"Bring it in ladies," she greets while motioning us to make a tight huddle. "Closer." We squeeze in even tighter. She raises her left hand to display a tiny new diamond on her ring finger.

"Engaged!" All eyes turn our way, but we don't hide the celebration this time. I see another bachelorette party and wedding in our future.

FORTY-ONE

You have to know your family tree extensively before dating in a small town. Be sure to look out for second and third cousins. Another of the 4,724 reasons I want to escape Athens.

I KNOCK LOUDLY on the door to Latham's barn. It seems silly to knock on a barn door, but I don't want to see anything I shouldn't. When they yell "come in," I only stick my head in. "Everyone decent?" Of course, Latham claims he's naked, Troy states he is never decent, and Winston laughs at their antics.

"I'm doing my maid-of-honor duties and ensuring we are all ready to begin in ten minutes." I take in their appearance. They seem to be dressed and ready.

A stall door opens. "How do I look? I tried to match as best I could."

I stand frozen. I cannot breathe. I cannot speak. It's Hamilton. He's here at the wedding. He told me he couldn't make it. I didn't prepare for seeing my friend, the father of my child. I'm just frozen numb, I squeeze my eyes closed tightly.

"Breathe." Hamilton's hot breath prickles my neck.

My eyes fly open as I jump back. Unable to stop myself, I continue taking steps back until I collide with the barn door. I'm trapped. I can't leave. I can't ruin Adrian's wedding. I have a job to do. I'm the maid-of-honor. I have to be front and center. I can't avoid him.

"Hey, I'm not going to hurt you." Hamilton holds his hands palm-out in front of him. He doesn't approach.

I see hurt in his eyes. My reaction to his surprise is unexpected, and I've hurt him. The last thing I want to do is hurt Hamilton. Drawing on an inner strength I didn't know I had, I run to him.

Hamilton wraps me in his arms while whispering in my ear. "I missed you too much."

His warm breath on my neck, sends a chill down my spine.

He chuckles at my shiver. "I'm sorry I didn't visit you this winter." He clasps his hands over jaws; eyes staring through mine into my soul. "I'm sorry for hurting you and for scaring you just now." His lips place a soft kiss on the tip of my nose.

Wiping my tears, I pull back. I swat his chest several times. "You lied to me. You said you couldn't make the wedding. Why?"

Hamilton grasps my wrists tightly. "My plans changed at the last minute. Coach made a change to our pitching rotation, so I asked if I might take one day to attend the wedding. I barely had time to arrange a flight to Kansas City and a rental car." He releases my wrists, then wipes stray tears from my cheeks. "By the time I made it to I-35 you were already with Adrian; I thought it best to surprise everyone." He looks to the guys. "At least, they were happy to see me."

I scramble to gather myself. I need to be normal, or, at least, the Madison he remembers. "I'm happy to see you. I've dreamt of you visiting me so many times. I feared I was imagining you here. I thought I lost my mind, because you told me more than once you couldn't come today." It's not a lie.

"Madison," Latham calls for my attention. "Rumor has it five females were found skinny dipping at a lake in Livingston County after midnight a couple of weeks ago. You wouldn't happen to know who they were, would you?" He folds his arms over his chest, tilts his head, and wears a knowing smile.

"I heard the Livingston County Sheriff's Department received a call and forced the girls from the lake then transported them to the county jail." Troy's love for law enforcement ensures he knows everyone in the field in a five-county area. I don't doubt he heard every little detail. "I can't wait to go on calls like that."

I stand stone-faced, letting nothing show. "Guys, I live in Columbia not Livingston County." I walk confidently in a circle around them. "If Bethany and I were picked up and booked for skinny dipping, we would never be able to attain our teaching licenses. And, you know Adrian has a big mouth. There is no way she would be able to keep such a juicy secret." I waggle my index finger at all of them. "What happens at the bachelorette party remains at the bachelorette party, and a public-nudity-with-trespassing arrest would not remain at the bachelorette party." I shrug and smirk.

"A friend of mine told me that some women crashed a bachelor party the same night in Daviess County." Troy claims. "They did a striptease and gave lap dances at a bar hosting a private party." His eyes scrutinize my face for any sign of guilt. "The women wore Zorro-like masks. Apparently, they were very hot and put on quite a show."

"C'mon! Sweet Salem crashing a party, stripping, and giving lap dances?" I scoff. "That I would pay good money to witness. As for the rest of us, those men only wish we would crash their party. There wouldn't be a dry fly in the place when we left." A maniacal laugh escapes me. "Are you really so desperate to know what we were up to that you would believe such wild stories?" I glance from man to man.

"Now, if you are done grasping at straws, we have a wedding to attend." I use my teacher voice to inflict guilt upon them. When they nod, I continue. "I'll let Adrian know you are ready and will meet us at the altar. Bye, gentlemen."

I walk from the barn, a cocky smirk upon my face and confidence in my shoulders and steps. Rumors about our activities have spread far and wide. The guys only wish they knew how ornery we were for ten hours that Saturday night.

Crap! Adrian is going to freak if I don't hurry back. I sprint back inside the house. I've been gone too long. I can't take the time I need to cope with Hamilton's arrival. I bury it deep for the moment. Hurrying inside the master bedroom, I lean against the door when I shut it.

"What's wrong?" Adrian's eyes bore into me.

I rescue my friend from her worst fears on her wedding day. "Nothing's wrong. The guys are ready," I proclaim. "Oh, and they have heard rumors of two of our activities from the bachelorette party. Wanna guess which two?"

Adrian, ever dominant, guesses first. "Soaping all the car windows at the dealership?"

I shake my head.

Savannah guesses next. "Placing the blow-up sex dolls in all the golf carts at the club?"

I chuckle.

"TP-ing the trees at the park?" Bethany asks, and I shake my head.

"Just tell us already," Adrian demands. "We don't have time to keep guessing. We have a wedding to attend."

As I touch up my eye make-up, I share what the guys asked, how I acted, and how I answered. We enjoy a long laugh. I remind the girls that we agreed not to share our adventures until after the reception tonight. We plan to keep the guys wondering for a bit longer. At the end of the reception, when the slideshow is viewed, our mugshots, along with several selfies from the bachelorette party, will be shared. While the guys remained on Latham's farm to play poker and party, we ventured to four counties, pulling many pranks and having loads of fun.

"Okay ladies," Adrian says. "It's time I get married so I can finally sleep with Winston tonight on our honeymoon." We laugh so hard our sides ache. I actually have tears. I've missed these friends.

FORTY-TWO

Deer season is like a holiday in Athens. This is one of the 4,724 reasons I want to escape this town.

―――――

ONE BY ONE, our friends step onto the porch, down the steps, and make their way to the barn. The faint strains of guitar drift from the front. I places a kiss upon Adrian's cheek before I follow the path of those before me.

As I descend the farmhouse steps, I realize I am walking toward the makeshift altar where Hamilton will be standing with Winston and the guys. I try my best to mask my fear. I knew someday I would be face to face with Hamilton. I was not prepared for it to be today.

I round the barn, taking in the first sight of Adrian and Winston's family and friends. They sit upon the quilts we cushioned the top of hay bales with to make the rows of seats. As the sun begins to fade in the evening sky, it shoots rays of light from behind the barn. Slowly, I walk down the makeshift aisle between the rows of hay bales; my eyes find Hamilton, standing tall in his jeans, shirt, and vest. Sans hat, his hair is a bit longer than I've ever seen. I long to run my fingers through his dark waves, blowing in the breeze. His warm, brown eyes are locked on me. His sexy smile melts my insides to pudding. I mentally slap myself. He's not here for me. As much as I desire another night in his arms, it won't happen. He did me a favor, nothing more. I had my one night with Hamilton—it's the only one I'll ever have. At least a little part of him will be near me always in Libby. I concentrate on my steps and assuming my place of honor.

Try as I might, I can't prevent my eyes from glancing towards Hamilton during the service or my mind from imagining this is our wedding. Hamilton's presence stirs up every memory of our night together, every fantasy I've had since that night and my hopes that maybe, someday, we might have a chance.

I pull myself together for Adrian. I listen to the minister. I focus on our place in the ceremony and the rest of my duties as her maid-of-honor. When Adrian doesn't repeat her vows for the minister, I realize she must be daydreaming, like I was. I nudge her side with my elbow. Adrian blinks from her thoughts, desperately trying to find where we are in our ceremony. They repeat their vows and exchange rings. When the minister says he may now kiss the bride, Winston bends her over backwards as his tongue invades her mouth. They enjoy a long, smoldering kiss amidst whistles, laughter, and cat-calls.

When they turn to face our guests as they are introduced as Mr. and Mrs. Hale, I hand Adrian her bouquet. With Winston's hand in hers, they run down the aisle. The crowd laughs at their escape.

Winston steals a kiss, full of promises for their time later tonight, before the entire wedding party catches up. As we join Adrian and Winston under the large tree and twinkle lights, our group of nine pull in tight. Adrian expresses her excitement that Hamilton made it to her wedding. I remind our group that guests are headed our way. After taking turns hugging the bride, we make the receiving line.

Hamilton stands next to me. I smile up at him. He places his hand on the back of my neck, pulling me in to whisper in my ear. "I can't keep my eyes off of you. Promise me we will find a moment alone tonight." His lips kiss my ear before he pulls away.

My attempt at control just evaporated. His hands, his touch, his lips, his kiss, I can't control my body's reaction to him. *A moment for what? To talk? To touch? To...*

Get a grip, Madison! I'm a grown ass woman. I'm a mother. I can't let my hormones control me. My heart can't handle another magical moment with Hamilton. I barely survived the first time. I need to think about Liberty. I need to get through tonight and head back to my new life in Columbia. I can't spend time alone with Hamilton, or I might tell him everything. I can't be the reason his dream, his career, ends. I need to leave Athens. In Columbia, I'm strong, and it's easier to remember why I'm keeping my secret from everyone. I must avoid him the rest of the night. I'll glue myself to the bride—it's my duty after all.

As we greet and thank each of the guests, the lights inside the barn rafters and stalls come to life. I love the simplicity of Adrian's special day. They are relaxed and stress free as they enjoy the time with others.

We delight in an evening of laughter, photos, dancing, and toasts. Adrian poses for pictures with us girls. The five of us stand in identical dresses with fluffy tutu skirts. We wear a denim vest over ours and the matching boots finish off our ensemble. Next, the guys join us in their new jeans, matching plaid shirts, grey vests, and boots. Winston wears a white shirt with the same vest, jeans, and boots as the guys. We pose for a few pictures in the beautiful red barn with twinkling lights.

Crap! Hamilton is walking my way. I've successfully eluded him for the past two hours. I frantically scan the area for a maid-of-honor task.

"Let's dance." Once again, Hamilton's warm hand is on my wrist as he pulls me to the dance floor.

Focus, Madison. It's a slow song. Prepare to be in his arms. No swooning. We are just good friends. We are just good friends.

I place my left hand on his right shoulder as he places my right hand in his. He wraps a long arm around my waist to my back and pulls me tight. Friends don't dance this close. *What is the meaning of this?*

"I'm sorry I've neglected you while I focused on my career."

Hamilton's word causes me to lift my chin to make eye contact.

"It's no excuse. I know I've hurt you."

I shake my head, unable to reply.

"Seeing you, touching you, I can't believe I led myself to believe our texts and phone calls were enough."

He releases my hand to run his fingers through his dark brown waves. The same hair his daughter has. I style hers to keep the curl—he fights the curl to make waves. She has his eyes, his hair, his height, and his smile.

This line of thought is nothing but trouble. I attempt to gather myself and blurt the first thing that comes to mind. "Your hair is long. Are you striving for a man bun?"

Hamilton's head falls back in laughter. "It's your fault. You've denied me video calls for several months now. As my number one fan, it's your job to keep me presentable for the rest of my fans."

"I figure you have a new number one fan, and she urges you to grow your hair out." I've missed our banter.

"How many times must I tell you? If I don't have time to visit you in person, then I definitely don't have time for anyone else. There can only be one number one fan and that is you forever."

The song ends. I lead Hamilton to the bridal party table to join the rest of our gang. I look to Adrian. She signals it is indeed time for the video presentation. I know she longs to jump Winston as soon as possible. I've already made her wait thirty minutes after her requested time to end the reception.

The guests react to the baby pictures, school photos, and casual pictures of our group of friends. A slide reading "The Bachelorette Party" causes gasps and groans.

Winston whispers in Adrian's ear that finally he will know the truth while wrapping his arms tightly around her waist. The wedding party surrounds them. The comments from the guys are exactly the reaction we hoped for. First, our mug shots are shared. I smile, recalling the deputies' agreement to treat us like criminals for a while. We were caught trespassing and skinny-dipping, but no charges were filed. When we shared, we were a bachelorette party, they offered to help us make memories to last a lifetime.

One thing is for sure; I can plan a perfect bachelorette party. We've always partied and had fun. However, that night, we did things we will brag about well into our golden years.

With the final slide reading, "And they lived happily ever after," the guests cheer. Winston and Adrian promptly make their way to the loft of the barn as it is announced all single men and women should gather just outside the barn doors. Winston removes Adrian's garter with his teeth. He shoots it from the loft to the gentlemen below. It lands in Latham's hands. Next, Adrian turns her back and throws the bouquet to the single ladies. Bethany pushes and shoves to catch it as the crowd laughs at her antics.

They climb down, exiting the barn through a tunnel of extended arms and sparklers. It feels like they are running through a field of lightning bugs as they make their way to Winston's truck and pull away.

Their wedding day was perfect. Winston is everything Adrian desires in a husband. It's funny how he's always been in her life. One day, it changed. Suddenly, Winston was more than her friend. He stirred desires within her and made her dream of a future together. Now that they are married, and their businesses are strong, they will start a family in their beloved small town of Athens.

THE EVENING HAS ENDED. I nervously say goodbye to many of the guests as they exit the barn. I am acutely aware of Hamilton, standing by Latham, near the barn doors. As he chats with Latham, his eyes remain on me. *How can I elude him on my way to my car?*

Adrian's mother and father wrap me in hugs and thank me for all my help with the wedding. They invite me to brunch in the morning, but I confess I must return to Columbia tonight, claiming I have a project I need to spend all of tomorrow on for class. I bid them goodbye, noticing that Hamilton vacated his post at the barn door.

"Driving in the dark?" Hamilton's deep voice asks from behind me. "You should stay at my mom's and leave early in the morning. I don't like the thought of you driving three hours this late at night." He tucks a stray tendril behind my right ear.

"I'm much too excited to sleep. It's a group project, and my partner is meeting me at nine in the morning at Alma's; so I need to pick up the house in the morning." I lie more and more each day. It started with me keeping my pregnancy a secret and developed into multiple lies to continue my charade. "What time is your flight?"

"My flight to Philadelphia leaves at 2:30 a.m." He runs his hands through his hair and over his face. "I really should be heading out now to ensure I get the rental returned, and I get through airport security."

I nod. I attempted to avoid him all evening, and now I don't want him to go.

"Come here, you." His open arms invite me for a hug. "I promise I'll arrange a visit after the season ends. I can't take another winter without spending time with you." He kisses the top of my head.

It takes all I have to keep it together.

He holds me at arm's length. "Goodbyes never get easier, do they?"

I shake my head.

Hamilton insists on escorting me to my car. We happen to be parked near each other in the front yard of the house. We quickly say our goodbyes, and he follows me down the gravel road and on the blacktop. When we meet the highway, he flashes his lights at me while we are at the stop sign. In my rear-view mirror, I see him exit his rental.

Outside my door, he prompts me to roll down my window. In the blink of an eye, his large shoulders enter my car. His lips smother mine. In his kiss, I feel all the emotions I hid inside for him.

Pulling away he smirks. "Eleven months seemed like an eternity away from you. Drive careful. I love you."

I watch in my mirror as he trots back to his car. Unsure what to do, I slowly pull onto the highway headed east. In my mirror, I watch his taillights as he drives west.

DURING MY THREE-HOUR drive to Columbia, my thoughts attempt to process the current state of my life. I'm nowhere near where I planned to be. My life looks nothing like I planned my senior year of high school.

The year following my high school graduation was nothing like I planned. Although I am seeking my teaching degree, Hamilton is not attending college with me. After asking my favor of him, I'm not sure if we are still friends or if we are more. With the birth of Liberty, my future goals seem to be morphing more and more by the day. I miss my friends in Athens and the life we all once shared.

Caring for Liberty helps distract me from the guilt of keeping the secret from Hamilton, his family, and our friends. Motherhood is more magnificent than words could ever describe. I can't regret the night with Hamilton as it gave me the greatest gift. A piece of him lives with me in our daughter.

Alma, Liberty, and I continue to watch every game of Hamilton's.

During my pregnancy, I recorded fifty-two videos in the digital journal for Hamilton and continued after Libby's arrival. I realize it will never make up for the time I kept from him.

Later this summer, I have tickets for Alma, Liberty, and me to see

Hamilton pitch against my favorite team in St. Louis. We will enjoy a mini-vacation while I record many moments for him.

It's not time to share my monumental secret. I will continue to ask for Alma's help in caring for Libby when my friends call. I need her to care for Libby when I attend celebrations back in Athens. I'm beginning to accept that I am not free from the pull of the small town of Athens. As my friends will always call it home, I will return from time to time.

With Alma's help, I can continue living one life in Columbia while pretending I live a different life for those in Athens. It's not easy, but Hamilton's career in Major League Baseball is worth it. I dream of the day I reveal Liberty to Hamilton and my friends, but, at least for the remainder of this baseball season, we need to remain in our own little bubble of secrets.

I'm glad Hamilton attended Adrian and Winston's wedding. I've missed him. Our continued calls and texts, while keeping us in touch aren't the same as seeing each other. I anticipated awkwardness the first couple of times I was in his presence after giving birth to Libby. I was not prepared for his actions today. He misses me, he misses touching me, he misses kissing me, and he loves me. I have no idea where this might lead, but a spark of hope lies within me that we will become more than friends.

When my enlightening drive ends as I pull into Alma's driveway, I smile. I'm happy with my life as I complete my degree. I have many blessings. I enjoy my classes. I belong to a caring and active church family. I am grateful for the time I spend with Alma, her family, and McGee. My biggest blessing of all is a healthy daughter and a renewed hope that in the next year I may unite her with her father.

My life is truly blessed.

THE END
ADRIAN FOUND HER HAPPY ENDING.

Madison's journey continues in Dusty Trail to Nowhere, Country Roads #2.

TRIVIA:

1. Athens, Missouri is a fictitious town. There was once a township of Athens, but I could find no town.

2. The first and last names of *ALL* characters in this book are the names of towns in Missouri. (Except McGee the dog.)

3. I write steamy romance as Haley Rhoades and children's books under the name Gretchen Stephens.

KEEP IN TOUCH

Keep up on the latest news and new releases from Brooklyn Bailey

Please consider leaving a quick review by using the links at the end of About the Author page.

ABOUT THE AUTHOR

Brooklyn Bailey's writing is another bucket-list item coming to fruition, just like meeting Stephen Tyler, Ozzie Smith, and skydiving. As she continues to write sweet romance and young adult books, she also writes steamy contemporary romance books under the name Haley Rhoades, as well as children's books under the name Gretchen Stephens. She plans to complete her remaining bucket-list items, including ghost-hunting, storm-chasing, and bungee jumping. She is a Netflix-binging, Converse-wearing, avidly-reading, traveling geek.

A team player, Brooklyn thrived as her spouse's career moved the family of four, fifteen times to four states. One move occurred eleven days after a C-section. Now with two adult sons, Brooklyn copes with her newly emptied nest by writing and spoiling Nala, her Pomsky. A fly on the wall might laugh as she talks aloud to her fur-baby all day long.

Brooklyn's under five-foot, fun-size stature houses a full-size attitude. Her uber-competitiveness in all things entertains, frustrates, and challenges family and friends. Not one to shy away from a dare, she faces the consequences of a lost bet no matter the humiliation. Her fierce loyalty extends from family, to friends, to sports teams.

Brooklyn's guilty pleasures are Lifetime and Hallmark movies. Her other loves include all things peanut butter, *Star Wars*, mathematics, and travel. Past day jobs vary tremendously from a radio station DJ, to an elementary special-education para-professional, to a YMCA sports director, to a retail store accounting department, and finally a high school mathematics teacher.

Brooklyn resides with her husband and fur-baby in the Des Moines area. This Missouri-born girl enjoys the diversity the Midwest offers.

Reach out on Facebook, Twitter, Instagram, or her website...she would love to connect with her readers.

amazon.com/~/e/B0B57RYXZ2
goodreads.com/brooklynbailey
bookbub.com/authors/brooklyn-bailey
instagram.com/brooklynbaileyauthor
facebook.com/BrooklynBaileyAuthor
twitter.com/brooklynb_books
pinterest.com/haleyrhoadesaut

Made in the USA
Middletown, DE
15 November 2024